Penelope did not wish to go to the salon with Mr. Talbot. Not when her feelings were in such a muddled state as they were just now. She had been certain, for so long, that she never wished to marry, But Mr. Talbot's kisses were changing everything.

They were meant to deceive her, and instead they were touching her heart and soul in a way she had not known possible. She found herself wanting to kiss Mr. Talbot again. Not that she would, she told herself. And yet, just the wanting appalled her. Was she a fool for feeling this way about a man who could not love her? And what about his kisses? And her response to them? Or her secret hope that he would kiss her again.

Was there something wrong with her that she should wish for such a breach of propriety? Or did other young ladies feel this way as well? She had to collect her thoughts. Meanwhile, she could dream of the kisses Mr. Talbot had given her. And imagine that she was kissing him back. Again . . .

An
Outrageous
Proposal

April Kihlstrom

A SIGNET BOOK

SIGNET
Published by the Penguin Group
Penguin Putnam Inc., 375 Hudson Street,
New York, New York 10014, U.S.A.
Penguin Books Ltd, 27 Wrights Lane,
London W8 5TZ, England
Penguin Books Australia Ltd, Ringwood,
Victoria, Australia
Penguin Books Canada Ltd, 10 Alcorn Avenue,
Toronto, Ontario, Canada M4V 3B2
Penguin Books (N.Z.) Ltd, 182-190 Wairau Road,
Auckland 10, New Zealand

Penguin Books Ltd, Registered Offices:
Harmondsworth, Middlesex, England

First published by Signet, an imprint of Dutton NAL,
a member of Penguin Putnam Inc.

First Printing, July, 1998
10 9 8 7 6 5 4 3 2 1

Copyright © April Kihlstrom, 1998
All rights reserved

Chapter 1

The Honorable Geoffrey Talbot gazed wistfully across the room. "That is the woman I wish to marry," he said.

Reggie Hawthorne leaned around to see who his friend was staring at. When he did, he burst into laughter.

"Oh, hey, that's a good 'un," he said with a snort. "Had me going, you did. Almost believed you were serious."

Talbot stared again at the woman in question. She had blond hair, hazel-colored eyes, and she was dressed in a gown of pale blue satin that became her amazingly well. She was, quite simply, a beauty though not in the common way. There was too much understanding in her expression and too much determination in the way she dealt with her suitors.

"I am not roasting you," he said reflectively. "Lady Penelope is, from all I have heard, precisely the wife for me. They say she is intelligent and interested in all sorts of odd things. And you can see she is quite pretty. What could suit me better?"

"P'rhaps, if you was wanting a wife," Hawthorne countered. "But why would you?"

Talbot smiled an oddly appealing smile. "My mother says it is time I was setting up my nursery. And it is the reason I came to London."

Hawthorne snorted. "So does my mother, but that don't mean I listen! Thought you was just saying that to please her. Can't mean you're serious?"

"Why not?"

"But Lady Penelope? You're a good fellow. Any number of other ladies would be happy to marry you."

"But I want Lady Penelope."

"Can't want her. Don't you know what they say about her?" Reggie protested.

"They say she is a bluestocking," Geoffrey replied. "They mean it to be a pejorative term, but I think I should like a wife who was a bluestocking. She would understand about my experiments. And a woman that intelligent would be most unlikely to enact me Cheltenham tragedies if she did not get her own way. I should be able to live my life just as I choose and still produce an heir."

Hawthorne cast his eyes upward. He was no longer laughing. "You're serious!" he exclaimed in a shocked voice. Then, vehemently, he began to shake his head. "No, it won't do. Put it right out of your mind."

The same sweet smile as before crossed Geoffrey Talbot's face as he teased his friend. There was a twinkle in his eyes as he said, "No, Reggie, I've made up my mind. I like the girl and I'm going to marry her."

"Oh, no you're not," Hawthorne said, still shaking his head. "Lady Penelope is the Earl of Westcott's daughter. Last of five sisters. And she ain't going to marry anyone. Ever. Everyone knows it because she's taken such pains to tell 'em so. Call her the Ice Princess, they do. Any number of wagers made at White's by fools who thought they could persuade her otherwise. Don't wish to see you doing the same."

"Oh, I shan't," Talbot said calmly.

Hawthorne sighed. "You still mean to go after her, don't you? Even after all I've said?"

Talbot nodded. "Do you not see? Surely Lady Penelope is so averse to marriage because she fears no man can or will understand her. Or her taste for intellectual matters. But I shall. And once she realizes that, what possible objection can she have to me?"

Hawthorne glared at his friend. "It only wanted that!" he said. "Very well. Go to the devil, then. But mind you remember, when she sends you to the rightabout, that I warned you."

Talbot shook his head, still smiling. "When have you ever known me to fail at anything?" he asked. "I've made up my mind. I shall marry Lady Penelope."

"You don't know anything about doing the pretty with the ladies," Hawthorne said, a hint of desperation in his voice. Then, abruptly, he stared at the glass in Talbot's hand and gave a sigh of relief. "Had too much to drink, that's it. Bosky. Three sheets to the wind. No sense in arguing now. Try again in the morning. You won't be so stubborn then. Come to your senses on your own, most likely, and I won't need to say a thing."

Geoffrey's eyes danced with merriment. "Quite right. No need at all," he agreed amiably.

Reggie Hawthorne shook his head. "Don't believe me, but it's true," he said fervently. "You'll see."

Geoffrey didn't answer but merely set down his glass and stalked off in the direction of Lady Penelope. Reggie closed his eyes, unable to bear the thought of watching the disaster about to unfold. One word, one hint, of Talbot's intentions, and the Westcott beauty would humiliate the man in front of all of the *ton's* finest families.

When no sounds of either laughter or anger reached his ears, Reggie risked opening his eyes again. He was just in time to see an astonishing sight. Lady Penelope gave her hand to Talbot and he led her onto the dance floor as the strains of a waltz began. Frantically, Reggie looked around for a waiter and a glass of something more to drink. Somehow, before the evening was over, he had a feeling he was going to need several more of these.

Talbot was quixotic, and Hawthorne had always known it. But even for him there ought to be some limits to his madness! And what Lady Talbot was going to say about the matter, he didn't even want to consider.

No, dash it all, it wasn't right, having to watch one's closest friend heading for a downfall at the hands of someone like the Ice Princess, Lady Penelope.

But Lady Penelope wasn't thinking of downfalls at the moment. Instead she was confused. She had granted Mr. Talbot a waltz thinking it would give her the quickest opportunity to give him a strong set-down. But he was offering her no chance to do so. He held her very correctly at arm's length and made no attempt to pay her improper compliments, as some gentlemen had been known to do.

Usually gentlemen tried to draw her closer but Mr. Talbot seemed almost to wish the distance were even greater. Nor did he seem eager to engage her in conversation. But if he felt that way, why, then, had he asked her to dance? In spite of herself, she began to be intrigued. She tried to remember what she had heard about the man as she waited for him to say something, anything to her.

Finally, Penelope could stand it no longer. She was the daughter of an earl and when she was intrigued, she simply asked whatever it was she wished to know.

"You are Lady Talbot's son?"

He inclined his head.

"You live in the country?" she persisted.

Again he inclined his head. Penelope began to feel annoyed. She was trying to be nice to him. With some asperity she asked, "And I suppose you are also the Mr. Talbot who has twenty thousand pounds a year?"

Now that got a reaction, Penelope thought with a shiver of satisfaction. His own eyes narrowed and he looked about to snap at her. Instead, he caught himself, his eyes widened again, and an almost mischievous look crossed his face. A moment later, she was sure she was mistaken.

Solemnly he told her, "My dear, Lady Penelope, I do

hope you will not tell the other young ladies of your acquaintance that little detail. Or"—he added as an afterthought—"their mamas."

"I should think they already know," Penelope answered tartly. Then, unwillingly, she said, "Why don't you want them to know?"

He shuddered. He distinctly shuddered. And closed his eyes for a moment before he looked down at her. His voice dropped so low that no one nearby could overhear, and in spite of herself, Penelope leaned closer so as not to miss a word of what he had to say.

"Surely, Lady Penelope, you of all people understand? I have distinctly been told that you are not dangling after a husband. And yet I know you have been subject to just the sort of impertinence one dreads, simply because you are considered an excellent catch."

Was he roasting her? Penelope frowned as she tried to decide. He looked at her with wide, innocent eyes and added, "That is to say, I could not be mistaken, surely? You are not dangling after a husband after all, are you?"

Penelope nearly gasped at the audacity of his question. An angry glint lit her eyes as she demanded, "Do you mean that you only asked me to dance because you think I don't want a husband?"

There was an odd look in his eyes. And an even odder note to his voice. As though he invited her to see them both as kindred spirits. Kindly he said, "Surely you chafe, just as I do, to always be told it is your duty to marry? To have your mama watching to make certain you are nice to potential partners? I am very sorry if I have offended you, but I thought you would understand."

There was such wistfulness in his voice that Penelope was moved despite herself. "I do know how it is," she said with quick sympathy. "But I thought it was only myself, and other girls, who were put under such pressures. I know gentlemen are also told it is their duty to marry, but surely no one can really force you to do so."

His lips twitched and she had the oddest impression that he wanted to burst out laughing. "Lady Penelope," he said fervently, "you have never met my mother!"

Which was very odd because Penelope most certainly had met Lady Talbot and she seemed the kindest, most gentle of women. But perhaps she was different toward her son?

"So you asked me to dance knowing I wouldn't set my cap for you?" Penelope said encouragingly.

"Precisely! What I admire most of everything I have heard about you, is that you have such an excellent mind," he said, whirling her about the dance floor. "I knew I could not be mistaken in thinking you would understand."

He beamed at her and Penelope was conscious of a certain degree of pleasure at having his approval. With any other gentleman, such a shaft of feeling would have alarmed her, but with Mr. Talbot there could be no cause for concern. Unlike the other callow fellows who were always dangling after her, he had no designs on her person or her fortune.

Penelope racked her brain for something she might have heard about him, something she could say that would be kind. "I have heard you have a number of fascinating hobbies," she said.

He grimaced. "Eccentric," he said wryly, "that's the word you've heard about me, isn't it? I have a laboratory on my estate and I've blown up two outbuildings already. Plus I like to visit museums and travel and look at dusty old places and things."

"Well, yes," she allowed, "but as I think I should like those things as well, if I were ever allowed to pursue such interests, I can scarcely fault you for that."

Now he looked at her with such warmth, such a smile in his eyes as well as on his face, that Penelope did feel a sense of alarm. She tried to draw back, forgetting they were in the middle of the dance floor with a hundred pairs of interested eyes on them.

He had not forgotten, however, and did not let her go. Instead he smoothly waltzed her to the edge of the dance floor, near where her mother and aunt stood waiting.

There he released her, retaining only a grip on her hand as he bowed and said, in a halting voice, "Thank you for your kindness to me, Lady Penelope. I hope we may meet again."

And then, although it was what she had wished, Penelope found that for the first time she could ever recall, she felt a distinct sense of loss at having a dance end early.

But before she could protest, or indeed say anything, Penelope was surrounded by delighted suitors, all of whom wished to finish out the waltz with her. She chose one at random and determinedly did not look back at Mr. Talbot. Had she done so, she might have been even more alarmed by the gentle, understanding smile on his face. She would certainly have wondered what caused it and worried what it meant.

As it was, she was distracted and answered at random all the other gentlemen who danced with her for the rest of the evening. In doing so she caused even more alarm and disappointment than usual. But Penelope could not help herself. She kept wondering why Mr. Talbot did not ask her to dance again.

Geoffrey Talbot saw Hawthorne moving toward him in a most determined way. He smiled seraphically and greeted Reggie amiably.

"Isn't she beautiful?"

"Yes, and I saw the way she abandoned you to dance with someone else," Hawthorne said grimly. "Told you that you didn't know how to do the pretty. Now will you understand you had best set your sights on someone else? Not that I think you need to set your sights on anyone," he added hastily, "but if you are determined to set up a household and your nursery, at least choose someone who likes men."

"I abandoned her," Geoffrey retorted. At the look of disbelief on Hawthorne's face, his own went sober. "Yes, I know what it might have looked like, but I did. All part of my plan, you know. Strategy."

Hawthorne threw up his hands in disgust. "If you are going to talk nonsense then I wash my hands of you."

The twinkle returned to Geoffrey's eyes. "Really? A pity. Then you won't, I collect, accompany me to the Westcott household tomorrow when I ask Lady Penelope to go out riding with me?"

Hawthorne's only answer was to reach for another glass of wine and shudder.

Chapter 2

Penelope would not admit, even to herself, that she was watching for Mr. Talbot the next afternoon. Or that she had dressed with special care, in a cambric gown of green that favored her, simply because she thought he might come. Still, she could not help looking up as each new caller was admitted, nor entirely conceal the disappointment she felt when none of the gentlemen was he.

She was abrupt with her admirers. As usual, that only seemed to encourage them even more. Would they never learn? Had they no pride? Penelope was heartily sick of every one of them.

Once she caught her mother's eye and hastily looked away. Aunt Ariana shook her head in patent disapproval. A lecture would certainly be forthcoming regarding her rudeness to her guests, once all the gentlemen left, but Penelope could not bring herself to care. The only person to have caught her interest in months was not here.

Then it happened. Mr. Talbot was announced and Penelope almost smiled before she caught herself. Perversely her sentiments underwent a change and she turned the smile into a disdainful scowl. If Mr. Talbot had chosen to call upon her, she told herself fiercely, then he was no better than any of the others. She would not be kinder to him than to anyone else.

But Lady Talbot sailed in, hard upon Mr. Talbot's heels, looking almost angry, and Penelope felt a twinge of sympathy despite herself. So that was why he was here. Well, she knew better than most what it was like to have to dance to one's parent's tune. So she did smile at him, after all, when he bowed over her hand.

Lady Talbot favored her with a thorough, appraising look that held more steel than Penelope recalled. She smiled back, and felt Mr. Talbot squeeze her hand in gratitude.

Which was the moment when Penelope realized he was still holding her hand and she instantly pulled it free. He drew up a chair beside her and hemmed and hawed as he tried to engage her in conversation. She noted that Mr. Talbot was as bad at such things as she was and she felt even more kindly toward him. Particularly when Mama and Aunt Ariana began to quiz the poor fellow.

"And how long have you been in London, Mr. Talbot?"

"One week, Lady Westcott."

"How long do you plan to remain?"

"Uh, that is, my plans are not—I—er—indefinitely, Lady Brisbane?"

"Perhaps, Geoffrey, you would care to ask Lady Penelope if she would like to go for a drive in your curricle," Lady Talbot said, leaning forward.

Mr. Talbot recoiled. Penelope definitely felt him recoil beside her. He glared at his mother.

"I could not possibly impose upon Lady Penelope," he said evenly. "Perhaps she has other plans."

That set the other gentlemen in the room snickering. Penelope's temper was promptly roused in his behalf. She turned to Mr. Talbot and said quite clearly, "Why, Mr. Talbot, I should be delighted to go for a drive in the park with you this afternoon."

Instantly there were objections from Penelope's other admirers.

"Lady Penelope never goes for a drive in the park!"

"Unfair, Talbot!"

"Please, Lady Penelope, if you wish to ride with someone, ride with me. I shall even let you handle the reins."

This last was said with a hint of desperation and Penelope regarded the speaker coolly. "I doubt that, Lord Featherwill. You would never risk your cattle in such a way and I should not dream of asking you to do so. No, it is Mr. Talbot who shall drive me round the park this afternoon. Shall we say at four, Mr. Talbot?"

"Penelope!" her mother remonstrated. "It is for Mr. Talbot to settle upon a time."

But Mr. Talbot only smiled warmly at her and then said to Lady Westcott, "I should be happy to call for Lady Penelope at four."

Then he added a look of gratitude that made Penelope smile, actually smile, a genuine smile at him. The poor man! He was clearly as uncomfortable as she was with all this nonsense, and she immediately decided to set him at ease as much as she could.

Under the circumstances, she was not in the least surprised to see him take his leave the moment it was proper to do so. Nor did she miss the look his mother gave him. No doubt he would have to suffer from a lecture all the way home just as she so often did.

Penelope was quite correct. Geoffrey did have to suffer a lecture on the way back to his London town house.

"That was the most absurd and dismal performance I have ever witnessed," Lady Talbot said tartly. "I don't suppose you are going to tell me what is going on? Or why I had to be dragged to the Westcott household today?

"Not that I mind, you understand. It is simply that I have never in my life seen you behave as clumsily as you did today. And I am not certain I like acting out someone else's script. Did you have to cast me as the overbearing mother, insisting you take Lady Penelope for a drive? Mind you, I am pleased to see you taking an interest in someone. It is good practice for you, for the day when you find someone you could feel a *tendre* for, and that is the only reason I agreed to do as you asked."

Completely unrepentant, Geoffrey grinned at his mother. "Well, I could have gone alone," he said meekly, "but I thought that you ought to have a chance to see Lady Penelope before I ask her to marry me."

"I have seen Lady Penelope before—Marry?" Lady Talbot shrieked as she realized what he had just said. "You plan to marry the girl? Have you lost your wits? She is a confirmed spinster! She hates men! She is out of the question! Entirely out of the question."

Geoffrey merely waited until his mother ran down. As abruptly as she began her tirade, she ended it. Then she stared at him shrewdly and said, in a perfectly normal voice, "Well, I presume you have a plan and this afternoon's performance was part of it. So tell me, how precisely do you mean to woo and win the Westcott chit? Throw her off guard with this nonsense and then abduct her? Am I to wake up one morning and discover you've run off to Gretna Green with the girl?"

Geoffrey sniffed. "Just for that slander, Mama, I am not going to tell you a thing."

He listened to another tirade and finally relented. "Very well, Mama, here is my plan," he said, leaning toward her. "Lady Penelope is afraid of men. Or marriage. I am not entirely certain which. Perhaps both. I am certain, however, that any man who approaches her openly, as a suitor, is instantly rebuffed. So I shan't. At least, I shan't approach her as a willing suitor."

"Well, then, what do you plan to do?" Lady Talbot asked warily, knowing her son only too well. "And what further part are you going to ask me to play?"

Geoffrey leaned back and crossed his arms over his chest. "I mean to tell Lady Penelope that she needn't fear me for the best of reasons. I shall tell her I am as opposed to marriage as she is. That I am only pretending to court her because you are such a dragon that I dare not refuse openly your command to try to find a wife."

That, of course, set off another tirade, with Lady Talbot wringing her hands and moaning about reputations and their friends. But Geoffrey was unmoved. He had made his plans and he meant to carry them out. No matter how silly it made him seem. He said as much to his mother.

With a lopsided smile he took her hand in his. "You are the one who taught me that pride was foolish if it stood in the way of happiness. That it was wrong to worry more about what people might say, than what was right for yourself and those around you."

Her expression softened and she pulled her hand free to gently touch the side of his cheek. "Are you so certain this is right for you? And for Lady Penelope?"

Geoffrey nodded slowly. "I am. What other wife can you imagine for me, Mama? Some silly chit with more hair than wit?"

Lady Talbot sighed. "Of course not."

"And Lady Penelope?" he persisted. "What better husband for her than someone who will understand her thirst for knowledge? Her desire to learn? Who else will encourage her to do both?"

"Yes, but Geoffrey," his mother said, still troubled, "what about love?"

An angry, mulish look crossed his face. He looked as though there were several things he wished to say, but in the end he did not. He simply said tightly, "Lady Penelope and I are both too sensible to wish for something as foolish as love in a marriage. We both, I trust, understand all the pitfalls to be found when it occurs."

Lady Talbot looked at her son and considered several things she might say. In the end, she discarded all but one of her objections. She had, after all, had almost thirty years to learn how stubborn her son could be.

Softly she said, "I worry about you, Geoffrey. Yes, and Lady Penelope as well. What if she really doesn't want to marry you? Even after you point out all the advantages to her. You cannot marry her against her will."

For the first time, Geoffrey's smile wavered. "She is a very intelligent woman, Mama. It is just that all her other suitors have gone about it wrong, and were wrong for her," he said seriously. "Once she gets to know me, she is certain to see the advantages of such a match. And I intend to make certain she does get to know me, even if I must deceive her a little to do so."

"But she won't be seeing the true Geoffrey," his mother pointed out, troubled.

He hesitated, then shrugged. "She'll see the important things about me. The rest can come later, once she agrees to marry me."

Lady Talbot shook her head. "And if she does not? If, in spite of everything, Lady Penelope does not wish to marry you? What will you do then?"

Geoffrey leaned back against the squabs, supremely confident. "You worry too much, Mama. I assure you it will not come to that."

Lady Talbot rolled her eyes in disbelief.

Penelope was having an equally hard time of it. Her family was quite bemused by her sudden kindness toward Geoffrey Talbot and they wished to know what it was all about. She refused to enlighten them.

"It ought to be enough for you that I am not condemning the man out of hand," Penelope said with a sniff. "He is eligible. Of good birth. With some twenty thousand pounds a year, they say. You ought to be happy I am polite to him. Nothing beyond that is your concern."

This might daunt her mother. And even give her aunt, Lady Brisbane, pause. Neither, after all, wished to risk having Penelope change her mind, now that she was finally showing an interest in someone. Particularly someone who was, as she had pointed out, so entirely eligible.

And while the Earl of Westcott, her father, might have objected to this cavalier dismissal of his responsibilities toward his daughter, his wife silenced him with one minatory glance.

Miss Tibbles, Penelope's governess, however, was undaunted. She waited until she was alone with the girl and then she said, "You've some mischief in mind and you'd best tell me what it is. And don't try to tell me it is none of my affair. Until you are married and out of this house, you are, in part my responsibility. And I will not shirk it."

Tears, protests, tantrums would have been useless. Penelope tried none of them. Instead she came and put her arms around the governess and said, "Oh, Miss Tibbles, I do not mean any mischief! Truly I don't. But I have found someone as put upon as I am, someone as opposed to marriage as I am, and I only wish to be kind to him."

Miss Tibbles disentangled herself from Penelope's embrace and tried to regard the girl sternly. She could not do it. Instead she smiled wistfully, scarcely conscious that she did so.

In any of Lord Westcott's other daughters, Miss Tibbles might have found such speech a trifle ingenuous. But Penelope's greatest fault, and her greatest virtue, was that she was not in the least afraid to speak her mind. She said what she meant. Always.

"Dear child," Miss Tibbles said, dabbing at her eyes, "I had so hoped you would find yourself able to overcome this—this repugnance you have toward men. I assure you they are not all evil. Indeed there are many you might like quite well, if ever you once gave them a chance."

Penelope found it difficult to speak. "It is not the men, so very much, to whom I object," she said, trying hard to explain. "It is the notion of being married at all. You cannot understand, I know, but I find the thought of being married worse than anything."

Now Miss Tibbles's tears abruptly disappeared. There was a singularly fierce expression upon her face as she said, "*I* do not understand? *I*, who have had to work as a governess for the past eighteen years because no one would marry the daughter of a man who shot himself due to debts he could not pay? *I* do not understand the disadvantages of marriage? Perhaps not, but you, my child, do not understand the disadvantages attached to a female who is not married and cannot marry. It is very easy for you to whistle down the wind an eligible partner. There are far too many of us who can only wish we might have had the choice!"

And then, because she feared she would say things even more revealing, Miss Tibbles turned and fled the room. She walked, back stiffly straight, at a dignified pace, but it was a flight, nonetheless, and both she and Penelope took it as such.

Behind her, Penelope watched, open-mouthed, as Miss Tibbles disappeared. It had never occurred to her, before, to consider whether the woman found her circumstances congenial. She had never expressed discontent in Penelope's hearing before and so it came as a sharp surprise to the girl.

And for the first time, Penelope wondered if she was quite so certain of what she wanted, after all.

It was odd but Penelope had never stopped to think of what Miss Tibbles's life must have been like before she became a governess. Oh, she had told them stories from time to time, but that was not the same thing. Particularly as Penelope and her sisters had never known how much to trust what Miss Tibbles told them. After all, she delighted in telling stories that would reveal things she wished them to know, or to believe, or ways she wished them to behave.

Now, for the first time, Penelope had a great many questions she wished she could ask Miss Tibbles, but she didn't quite dare. It was not, precisely, that she feared being snubbed, for despite her brusque exterior, Miss Tibbles always tried to be kind to the girls. It was more that Penelope was not entirely certain she wished to know the truth. For that might have meant she would have to reconsider so much of what she believed to be true.

Chapter 3

Several hours later, Lady Westcott regarded her youngest daughter with patent affection. "You look so pretty in sprigged muslin," she said with a sigh.

Penelope kicked at her skirts and scowled at her mother. "Perhaps I should cry off," she said.

"No! You cannot! That is, surely you do not wish to disappoint Mr. Talbot?" Lady Westcott asked. "I thought you said you liked him? You were kinder to him than you usually are."

"That does it," Penelope said, rising to her feet and jutting her lower lip out mulishly. "I am not going out riding with Mr. Talbot. When he comes . . ."

But it was too late. Mr. Talbot was already being shown into the drawing room where Penelope waited with her aunt and mother. Which only went to show, she thought gloomily, that perhaps her older sisters were correct in saying one ought never to be ready when a gentleman came to call, that one ought to always keep him waiting.

Mr. Talbot came to an abrupt halt and his gaze seemed particularly perceptive as it rested on Penelope. "I collect I come at a bad time," he said quietly.

"No!" Lady Westcott cried.

"Of course not," Lady Brisbane said smoothly, gliding forward. "My niece is ready, as you can see, and quite eager for that drive around the park."

Penelope lifted her chin. "I have changed my mind," she said loftily.

But then he held his hand out to her. How dare he hold his hand out to her? How dare he look at her with such sympathetic understanding in his eyes? Or speak so softly and gently, one might even say meekly?

"Are you certain, Lady Penelope? I promise I shan't annoy you with useless chatter. You may ride beside me and not say a word, if that is what you wish."

"There now, you see? Nothing could be better!" Lady Brisbane said firmly. "Don't you agree, Delwinia?"

"I, uh, that is, yes, of course. How amiable of Mr. Talbot."

But Mama didn't look as if she thought it was amiable at all. She was looking at Mr. Talbot as if she thought he had lost his wits and as if she thought perhaps she ought to withdraw her approval of the outing. Perhaps that was what decided Penelope. If Mama disapproved, then she was most certainly safe riding out with Mr. Talbot.

Penelope withdrew her hand from his and started toward the door. "Very well, Mr. Talbot. I shall ride out with you. But not a word, mind you, not a word!"

He bowed and was silent as Penelope led the way out of the room. Too silent. But that, she told herself with a sniff, was precisely what she wanted.

Of course, by the time they had driven around the park twice with not a word said by Mr. Talbot, Penelope began to feel her patience wearing thin. Finally she could bear it no longer.

"Are you always this silent, Mr. Talbot?" she snapped.

He looked startled and then grinned. "I only meant to please you, Lady Penelope, or rather," he added hastily as an angry glint came into her eyes, "not to annoy you. I could see you were no more comfortable with this absurd ritual than I was. Which was why I asked you in the first place."

Stung, Penelope demanded, "What do you mean, sir? You sound almost insulting."

He coughed and risked rubbing his nose with one hand before he explained, an apologetic note in his voice, "It is just that Mama is so determined I should make myself agreeable to the ladies. Or at least one lady. Any one lady. But most young ladies are so eager for marriage that it is very disconcerting. Surely, you have felt the same, from time to time, with your suitors, Lady Penelope?"

"From time to time," Penelope agreed cautiously.

"There, you see. I knew you could not want another preposterous fellow annoying you. I knew I could safely drive you around the park and not have to worry that I was raising expectations in your mind."

Once again Penelope felt as though she had been vaguely insulted. Still, she could not help but agree with the sentiments Mr. Talbot had expressed.

Hesitantly, she said, "It is a trial when one has a matchmaking mama."

"Indeed. And I know I should not keep on annoying you with my attentions, but it is very hard to know what else to do!"

His sigh was so mournful that Penelope put a reassuring glove on his arm and said, "You may call upon me as often as you need to, in order to reassure your mama. I won't mind and I promise I shan't misunderstand."

Now he turned deep gray eyes upon her and a dazzling smile that caused her heart to beat disconcertingly faster. "Do you mean it, Lady Penelope? What a wonderful woman you are! Are you certain? I cannot think how to show you how grateful I am."

In spite of herself, Penelope smiled. "I am quite, quite certain, Mr. Talbot. We are fellow sufferers and must do what we can to help one another."

He looked much struck by her words and nodded vigorously. "That is just what I was thinking. How extraordinary! I had been dreading my time here in London but now, why, now I think I might almost be able to bear it!"

Not wishing to pry but unbearably curious, Penelope asked cautiously, "If you dislike London so much, then why are you here?"

Gloom set in upon his countenance once again. "Mama, of course. She will have it that it is time I set up my nursery. She insisted. If I had not come to London, she would have dragged some poor girl to my estate and you know how particular that would have looked. There would have been no escaping the parson's mousetrap then. Not by the time my mama was done with her scheming."

A tiny frown creased Penelope's forehead. "Your mama never seemed so . . . so scheming to me," she said. "I have not met her often, as she and my aunt are only slightly acquainted. Still, she seemed so amiable."

He nodded grimly. "Yes. That is precisely how she seems. Until she sets her mind upon something. Then she is still amiable but also immovable and somehow, in the end, one finds oneself doing just what she asked in the first place because it is useless to struggle against her. She never gives in. And she can make one's life so uncomfortable when she chooses to do so. I love her dearly, you understand, it is just . . ."

He allowed his voice to trail off. Penelope nodded and sighed. "My mama and papa can be just the same. And they have decided that since all my other sisters are married, it must be my turn. And nothing I say can persuade them I am not interested in marriage."

Mr. Talbot shook his head. "I feel for you, Lady Penelope. It is so difficult. I can, if all else fails, escape to the country. You, I fear, are more captive to your parents' wishes."

Penelope stared at him, thinking that here, at last, was one man who understood what she felt. He was also kind and she rated that quality highly, for far too many men and women she had met in London were not.

It was such a relief, she thought, to be able to enjoy the company of a man without the bothersome question of romance raising its head. So with a tiny sigh of relief, Penelope relaxed and asked Mr. Talbot about his interests. He, in turn, seemed eager to discover hers.

It was amazing how many they had in common and so lost were they in conversation that the park was all but deserted by the time Mr. Talbot abruptly pulled himself up short and said in dismay, "Good heavens! We have been out for more than two hours. Your mother will be most upset, I fear, and rightly so. Come, let me drive you home and explain."

Penelope shook her head, even as he headed for the gates of the park. "You must take me home, yes, but do not, I pray you, come inside with me. It will only add fuel to Mama's absurd expectations."

"But I cannot leave you to face her alone!" he protested with patent concern.

She patted his arm. "You are very kind to worry, Mr. Talbot," she said, "but I can handle Mama. And Aunt Ariana. And Papa."

He protested again, but in the end agreed to her wishes in the matter. If only her other suitors were so amiable, Penelope thought wistfully. But then perhaps that was the difference. Mr. Talbot was not a suitor. He was, like her, determined to remain unwed.

When they arrived at the town house, he handed her down and walked her up the steps but then left, at her command. Her last glimpse of Mr. Talbot, was his grin as he deftly wheeled his curricle away from the curb and into the late afternoon traffic.

Penelope smiled to herself and went inside.

Penelope Westcott would not have been nearly as happy with Mr. Talbot if she had seen the smug air that his smile took on the moment he rounded the corner and was safely away from Lady Brisbane's town house. Or the way he chuckled to himself.

And if she could have heard what he said to his friend, Reggie Hawthorne, later that evening when the two of them were sitting over an excellent port after dinner in Hawthorne's rooms, she would have been angry enough to want to box his ears.

"I tell you, I shall be betrothed to Lady Penelope before the month is out," Geoffrey predicted, taking a sip of the rich wine. "And married before the summer is over."

Reggie gasped and sputtered and hastily wiped his mouth with his napkin. "Married?" he squawked.

Geoffrey tapped his nose. "Told you I would be. Told you last night."

"But—but—you've only known her one day. Do you mean to say she's accepted you after only one day?" Reggie demanded.

Geoffrey shook his head. "Hasn't accepted me at all. Yet. And mind, not a word to a soul. But she will accept me. Betrothed before the month is out. And married, well, if not before the summer is over, then certainly before next year's Season comes around."

Reggie Hawthorne stared deep into his wineglass and then at Talbot. "Bosky. That's what you are. Bosky. Don't know what you're saying. 'Cause if you did, you would know it was nonsense."

Geoffrey merely smiled. "Not a word to anyone," he reminded his friend.

"Wouldn't think of it!" Reggie said fervently. "Mean to say, a lady's reputation at stake. And yours. Anyone heard what you've told me, they'd clap you up in Bedlam. And even if they didn't, why, you'd be the laughingstock of London. No, you can be sure I shan't tell a soul."

Geoffrey leaned back in his chair and smiled some more. "Do you know, I shall greatly enjoy it when you find a lady you wish to marry."

"Won't!" Hawthorne said firmly.

"Oh, yes you will," Talbot retorted with a grin. "Just wait until you meet the right lady and you will be as eager as I am to enter the parson's mousetrap."

"Never!" Reggie exclaimed, visibly revolted by the notion.

"Just wait," Talbot said with a devilish grin.

It delighted Geoffrey to think of Reggie succumbing to something like this. It really was nothing like what he had expected. But now that he was caught, he wished to see his friend caught as well. Never mind that had it been three years ago he, too, would have sworn such a thing was impossible. This was now and he had met his Waterloo and now he wanted to see Hawthorne meet his.

Reggie continued to grumble. "Ought never to have taken you to that ball last night. Ought to have known better. Keep you locked up with your books, that's what I ought to have done. Should have known that when a man ain't used to the company of ladies, he's likely to lose his head. Stands to reason, don't it?"

Talbot merely smiled and sipped his wine, his eyes twinkling with humor. "Don't worry about it," he advised. "You'll only get a headache if you do."

"Get much worse than that," Reggie grumbled. "You get in trouble and who will your mother blame? Me, that's who. Said so last time she saw me."

"She was roasting you," Geoffrey assured his friend, but it took some time and a few more glasses of wine before Reggie believed him.

Chapter 4

Lady Westcott paused in her sewing and let the handkerchief she was embroidering for Lord Westcott fall to her lap. Lady Brisbane noticed at once.

"Worried?" she asked, cocking a skeptical eye at her sister.

"Yes. No. Oh, I don't know, Ariana. Mr. Talbot has been so particular in his attentions of late and Penelope hasn't made the least push to send him to the right about. It has been three days already! She has never tolerated so impetuous a suitor for even half that long!"

The Earl of Westcott set down his paper. And Lady Brisbane set down her book. A pity, for it was one of her favorites. But family duty came first.

"Simple," Lord Westcott said airily. "Doubtless Penelope likes the fellow. Not a mystery at all."

"He could be right," Lady Brisbane agreed cautiously.

Lady Westcott rose to her feet and began to pace about the sunny parlor she loved so well. "Yes, of course Penelope likes Mr. Talbot. But what has that to say to anything? She has liked any number of young men, prior to this, and still not allowed any of them to court her."

As there was no denying this simple fact, neither Lord Westcott nor Lady Brisbane attempted to do so. Instead he picked up his paper again while she set her reading spectacles on top of the closed book, a sign that she had truly resigned herself to addressing the matter at hand.

"Perhaps it is time to speak to Miss Tibbles," she said.

For a moment it seemed that both Lord and Lady Westcott would object but then Lady Westcott nodded. "I suppose we must. Surely she knows something of Penelope's mind."

Lady Brisbane smiled sourly and merely rang the bell-pull in response.

Five minutes later, Miss Tibbles sat opposite the two ladies. Lord Westcott stood behind them and stared at the governess. She had a bewildered expression upon her face that none of them had ever seen before.

"I wish I were privy to Penelope's mind," she said, "but it is as puzzling to me as it is to you. Oh, she has not changed so much that she frets about what to wear when Mr. Talbot comes to call, but she does not privately abuse him, the way she has her other suitors. Nor does she make excuses not to come down, or make up scandalous nick-names for the fellow. She will not confide in me, however much I press her to do so. It is all beyond me."

Lady Brisbane repeated the theory she had concurred with before. "Perhaps Penelope genuinely likes Mr. Talbot."

"Yes, but I cannot think why," Miss Tibbles said with a frown. "He is handsome, of reasonable height, quite strong, I should think, and he looks at her in a way, when she is not looking, that by all past experience should have caused her to send him packing straightway. I simply do not understand it at all."

"Perhaps that is the answer," Lord Westcott said slowly. "Perhaps he only looks at Penelope like that when she isn't looking at him."

Both sisters started to object but didn't. Instead they looked at one another. It made sense.

"Let us hope, then, that he continues to show such good sense," Miss Tibbles said tartly, "and we may find Penelope married after all."

Penelope was not thinking about being married. She was thinking how nice it was to have someone to talk with who entered into all her sentiments exactly and who knew how to discuss subjects in an intelligent manner that did not require her to turn away unwelcome compliments.

Had she been of a mind to marry, she could, she thought, have done much worse than to choose a man like Mr. Talbot. But she was not of such a mind and, fortunately, neither was he. Penelope did spare a moment or two to wonder what it was that had set Mr. Talbot so against the institution.

That is to say, she understood the evils so far as they affected women, but it seemed to her that gentlemen only gained. However, even the slightest observation of society showed that most gentlemen did not think so. Whether it was because there was some factor she was leaving out or because they were too foolish to know their own good, she could not say.

Perhaps, the next time she saw him she could ask Mr. Talbot about this paradox. He had, after all, encouraged her to ask him anything, to talk of anything she wished. It was a wondrous change from her past experience and she could not seem to have enough of his company. For all that she loved her four sisters dearly, there was not a one who had the same scientific turn of mind that she did, the same love of learning just for learning. But Mr. Talbot did.

Nor did she ever have to worry that he would go beyond the line. Indeed, what set Mr. Talbot apart from others who did not wish for marriage was that he did not engage in pointless flirtation. Even those who were most opposed to the institution of matrimony seemed incapable of speaking with a woman without doing so. Only Mr. Talbot treated her as he might have treated another man.

Or so Penelope thought. And that, she told herself, was why she trusted him.

Geoffrey Talbot, of course, was very far from thinking of Penelope as another man. And the Westcotts were not the only ones who were concerned about this strange courtship. Lady Talbot eyed her son as he prepared to leave the house. He had come into the drawing room to take his leave of her.

"Lady Penelope again?" she asked shrewdly.

Geoffrey grinned at his mother. "Of course!"

Lady Talbot hesitated, then plunged in: "It is most unlike you, Geoffrey, to be so particular in your attentions. Oh, I know that you have said you mean to marry the girl, and I cannot object to someone with such impeccable breeding and fortune to recommend her. I even like Lady Penelope. As you yourself have said, she isn't a pea-goose without two thoughts to rub together, the way so many young ladies seem to be, concerned only with clothes and such. I shouldn't be able to abide that sort of daughter-in-law."

"Then what is the trouble?" Geoffrey asked shrewdly. "Changed your mind about my getting married, and setting up my nursery?"

Lady Talbot hesitated. "No. Not if you truly care for her and she cares for you. Then I should like it above all things. But does she care for you? I mean to say that you are taken with her, and may well succeed in your scheme, for you have always succeeded in any scheme you have undertaken, but what if you marry Lady Penelope? This blood-less match you have chosen seems so cold to me. I should hate to see you unhappy, Geoffrey, and I am so afraid you may be."

Talbot lost the impish smile and came to kneel beside his mother. He took both of her hands in his. "I know you are concerned, best of mamas, but I promise you that I know what I am about."

Lady Talbot thought fondly that it was almost impossible to resist Geoffrey's charm. From his dark blond hair to his fine gray eyes and his moderate height, there was nothing to cavil at in his appearance. Indeed, he drew many an admiring glance from the ladies.

With an effort she pulled her hands free, rose to her feet, and began to pace about the room. With the arrogance of one who has no need to be concerned over his consequence because it is so much a part of him, Geoffrey settled himself on the floor to watch her.

"Do you know what you are about, Geoffrey?" she demanded. "I worry, you see, because I think you will succeed and then both you and Penelope will suffer because of it. No, don't tell me how certain you are! It is and has always been your one failing, this arrogance that you know what is best. And so often you are right. But not always. And in this case, when it means being tied to someone else for the rest of your lives, well, I cannot be complacent."

Now Geoffrey rose to his feet and crossed over to his mother again. This time when he took her hands his voice was soft and serious. "I do understand your concerns, Mama. And perhaps you are even right. Very well, will it reassure you if I promise to cry off should I discover I have made a mistake? Even if it means disgrace?"

Lady Talbot tried to be harsh with her son, but she could not. She loved him too well and she was shrewd enough to understand that no words of hers could truly warn him of what lay ahead. Still she tried.

She lifted a hand and touched the side of his cheek. "Oh, Geoffrey, you have nothing to cry off from! But should you succeed and find yourself able to announce a betrothal, then cry off later, it is not only you who would be disgraced, but Lady Penelope as well. Why can you not let yourself look for someone who can and will love you?"

He was impatient, as she knew he would be. "This is all nonsense," he said. "I promise you, Lady Penelope will come to respect and admire me! There will be no reason to cry off and no one will be disgraced at all. As for love, well, I have told you what I think of that," he concluded grimly.

Lady Talbot stared into her son's eyes. Almost she wished Lord Talbot were here, but it would have done no good if he

were. He would be away at his clubs gaming, not here, caring what happened to his son. And his very face would remind Geoffrey of why he was unalterably opposed to love.
No, better that Lord Talbot was safely home in the country,
even if it meant she must cope with this dilemma alone.

"I worry," she said, "that it is my example which has put
you off the notion of love."

He did not contradict her.

"Very well, I understand why you do not wish for love,"
Lady Talbot said with a sigh, "but I wish I knew why Lady
Penelope was so opposed to it. I fear you are taking griev-
ous advantage of her."

Geoffrey felt his temper rising. "Do you think I am selfish, then, to want this marriage? That I am thinking only of
myself? You are mistaken, Mama! I wish it as much for her
sake as for mine."

He began to pace around the room, waving his arms as
he spoke. "Can you imagine how Lady Penelope must feel,
hedged about as she is, by a family that can conceive of
only one purpose for her? To become a wife and mother?"

"Yes, but—"

"I want to take her about, to salons, where she will meet
others who also wish to learn. Women who do not see their
roles confined to hearth and home! I would have her know
of women who have made scientific discoveries. Men who
have traveled where she has never been. Do you call me
selfish for that? For wishing to give her what she would
most want, could she obtain it for herself?"

He paused to stare fiercely at his mother, daring her to
contradict him.

"If you are right and this is what she would wish, why
then I think it very admirable of you," Lady Talbot replied
mildly.

"If?"

Now Lady Talbot spread her hands wide. "Well, how
can you be certain? Have you asked Lady Penelope?"

"No, but I know it from everything she has said about herself. From everything I have heard said about her," he countered, tilting up his chin.

"Well, perhaps you are right," Lady Talbot conceded, "but I should feel much better, you know, if you were to test your hypothesis by taking Lady Penelope to some of these salons. I should even be willing to act as chaperone and go with the pair of you, if you wish. But before, not after, you are married," she added. "If you are mistaken, you had best discover it as soon as possible."

Geoffrey grinned at his mother. "You are wonderful!" he exclaimed. "It will answer perfectly. The only difficulty will be in persuading Lord and Lady Westcott to let her go. It will be one more way to impress Lady Penelope that I am the very husband she should wish for."

A twinge of conscience struck Lady Talbot and she warned him earnestly, "None of this may work out as you wish, Geoffrey. I would not for the world see either you or Lady Penelope hurt."

"We shan't be," he said confidently. "It will all work out marvelously well, I promise you."

There was nothing more to say and Lady Talbot did not try. Instead she watched as Geoffrey finished his preparations and left the house. She wished she could go and speak with Lady Penelope honestly, but in truth a part of her hoped his campaign would be successful. She could not imagine a better wife for her son.

And yet she had her doubts. And her fears. Lady Talbot did not know where all this would lead, but she fervently hoped it would not end in scandal. She had had enough of that in her life already.

Still, she was pleased to know that Geoffrey had begun, already, to think of what would make Lady Penelope happy. She, of all people, knew how much it would matter if he tried.

Chapter 5

Reggie Hawthorne stared gloomily into his glass. "Married! M'best friend thinks he is getting married. It don't bear thinking of."

Hawthorne could not have known that Lady Penelope was nearby or he would never have spoken. But she heard him and halted, stunned, for she knew only too well, by now, that Hawthorne and Talbot were best friends. His next words confirmed her fear.

"Geoffrey and that Ice Princess. It don't bear thinking of at all."

Penelope felt the room spin and she had to grasp for the back of a nearby chair. Geoffrey? And the Ice Princess? He could only mean Talbot and herself. Up until this moment, she had known about and taken great pride in her nickname. But now it was being linked to his!

Anger replaced shock and Penelope looked about for Mr. Talbot. He had gone to fetch her a glass of something to drink. When he returned, she would give him the rough side of her tongue.

How dare he link his name with hers and bandy such nonsense about? And it must have been Talbot for Hawthorne would have believed it from no other source. At the very least he would have asked Talbot if it was true and he must have confirmed it.

Ah, there was Mr. Talbot now, weaving his way through the other guests. Penelope prepared herself to tell him precisely what she thought of his behavior.

* * *

Geoffrey Talbot was not prepared for the angry termagant who greeted him when he returned to where he had left Lady Penelope waiting. She took the glass from him and promptly threw it in his face, then stalked away. Talbot was too shrewd to try to follow. Instead he looked about for someone, anyone, to explain what had made her do such a thing. Unfortunately, by then, Reggie had already disappeared.

But he had answer enough when three people stopped him to ask if it was true that he and the Ice Princess were on terms that might lead to a betrothal, and another said that judging by the lemonade all over Talbot's shirt, he thought not. Someone, Geoffrey thought grimly, must have said the same sorts of things to Lady Penelope.

Well, he would take steps to remedy the disaster. Indeed, perhaps he could turn it to his benefit and persuade her to become betrothed even sooner. Fortunately for his friendship with Hawthorne, it did not occur to Geoffrey that it needed anything more than his constant attention to Lady Penelope to account for such impertinence.

The next day, Talbot was on Lady Brisbane's doorstep the moment it was proper to call. There was a look of grim determination on his face and while he greeted Lady Westcott and Lady Brisbane, he stalked straight to Penelope and said, bowing over her hand, "I shall be here at four o'clock to take you out driving."

"I shan't go," she said.

Geoffrey looked down at her. "I think you will."

And then he stalked away.

At four o'clock he arrived again at the Brisbane town house and was told that Lady Penelope was indisposed. Geoffrey was generally a very mildly tempered fellow. But now he smiled at the majordomo and said, pleasantly, "Pray tell Lady Penelope that she has five minutes to come down or I shall go up and fetch her myself."

Jeffries's only excuse for delivering the message, indeed for not having the fellow removed at once, was that despite his angry words, Mr. Talbot was a gentleman and one could see he would not truly go beyond the line of what was proper. Besides, Lady Penelope had been glad enough to see Mr. Talbot the day before and he knew that both her parents and Lady Brisbane were eager to see the girl wed and that they placed great hopes on his suit.

Penelope was not down in five minutes, but a petite older woman was. She found Geoffrey pacing in the foyer and turned her sternest gaze upon him. He found himself amused and waited as she tried to intimidate him.

"You are Mr. Talbot, I presume?" the dragon demanded.

Geoffrey bowed, his lips twitching with amusement.

"What is the meaning of your impertinent message to Lady Penelope?"

"I thought it was quite clear. Did I phrase things in such a way that they could be misunderstood?" he asked ingenuously.

"Do not play such games with me," the woman retorted grimly. "I am Miss Tibbles, her governess, and I will not stand for it! You know very well what I mean. Your message was impertinent and outrageous and I cannot permit my charge to obey it."

Geoffrey quirked one eyebrow. "Not even when I sent it up so that Lady Penelope would see me and I could apologize? Not even if it means I may bring her back from the ride betrothed to me?"

Miss Tibbles hoped she was a sensible woman. She hoped she always did what was best, what was proper for her charges. And she knew she should send Mr. Talbot away with a flea in his ear.

But, oh, how she was tempted to aid his cause. Lady Penelope, fifth daughter of the Earl of Westcott, had been the most difficult charge Miss Tibbles had ever undertaken in a career that specialized in difficult daughters. However outrageous the behavior of other daughters, they had at least always wanted to eventually marry.

Lady Penelope did not. She told them so, her parents and Miss Tibbles and her aunt, loudly and frequently. Mr. Talbot was the first suitor Penelope had even tolerated. And so, despite the outrageousness of his message, she was sorely tempted to abet his cause.

Fortunately for Miss Tibbles and her scruples, it was not necessary. Penelope must have been listening on the stairs for, the moment she heard Mr. Talbot say he might return with her betrothed to him, Penelope came clattering down the stairs, shrieking at Mr. Talbot.

"How dare you say such a thing? You are mad! I thought you different and you are not! I hate you, I hate you, I hate you!"

Before Penelope knew what he was about, and before Miss Tibbles could protest, even if she wanted to, Mr. Talbot had caught Penelope, swung her around toward the door, grabbed a wrap that the majordomo was expressionlessly holding out for the girl, and whirled her out the door.

After they were gone, Jeffries and Miss Tibbles stared at one another, openmouthed, for a very long moment. Then Miss Tibbles turned and marched back upstairs, ruthlessly, ineffectually, trying to suppress a bubble of mirth and hope that threatened to bring a smile to her stern face.

As for the majordomo, he hurried below stairs to convey to the others every detail of the delicious encounter. Not that he would gossip. Perish the thought! No, he would merely allow to be dragged out of him an explanation of the noise in the foyer that had ceased so abruptly and with such entertaining results.

In the curricle Lady Penelope settled the wrap on her shoulders more carefully and then crossed her arms over her chest. She would not, she decided, speak to Mr. Talbot. She would ride in mutinous silence and thus make very clear to him precisely how she felt. And if anyone saw her do so, all the better.

Tears threatened to spill out of her eyes as she thought of how Mr. Talbot had betrayed her and she had to blink them back furiously. She would not let him see he had overset her. She would not give him the satisfaction.

But it seemed Mr. Talbot did not wish to overset her. The moment they were inside the gates of the park, he set down his groom. Then he apologized. And very meekly, too.

"I am very sorry, Lady Penelope. I never meant for matters to go this far. I collect you have heard by now and I can only blame my mother."

"Your mother?" Penelope gasped in outrage. "What a bouncer! It was not your mother in the foyer of my aunt's house announcing that I would come back from this ride betrothed to you. Nor was it your mother I overheard at the ball last night saying that you and the Ice Princess were going to be married. I know very well that is what they call me. But it was your best friend who said we were to be married! And how could he have thought such a thing unless you told him so?"

He sighed. "Reggie? I ought to have known he wouldn't be able to keep his mouth shut. It must have been most upsetting for you," he said, as meekly as before. "And I feel dreadful over that. But it truly was my mother's fault. She was badgering me, mercilessly, to be married and finally I told her that you and I had come to an understanding. It was wrong of me, I know, but I couldn't think what else to say. And then Reggie Hawthorne came by and she told him. I came by today to explain and to apologize."

He paused and looked at her hopefully but Penelope resolutely stared ahead. "That does not explain your outrageous statement that we would come back from this drive betrothed," she said.

"I thought," he said, his voice cracking slightly, "that perhaps you might be willing to pretend we were betrothed, just for a little while. That is what I meant."

Now she did turn and look at him, with all the astonishment and wariness of one who finds herself with a madman.

"Have you lost your wits?" she gasped. "How could you possibly think I would be willing to pretend to be betrothed to you?"

He hesitated. His voice was meek, so very meek, as he said, "Well, it is just that I thought, you see, that it had worked so well with my mother, that it might help you to get some respite from the importunings of your family."

He paused and drew a deep breath. "It wouldn't be a real betrothal," he said. "After a month or so we would announce we had made a mistake and I would cry off. And then both my mother and your family would be at us again. But for that month or two we would have some peace."

"I—" Penelope opened her mouth and then closed it again. The notion was undeniably tempting.

"Of course, I see it will not do," Mr. Talbot said mournfully. "It would ruin both our reputations and then no one would want to marry us."

That settled it. Penelope turned to Mr. Talbot and placed her hand on his arm. "I'll do it!" she said, her eyes sparkling with mischief.

"No, no." Mr. Talbot shook his head. "I was wrong to suggest it," he said virtuously. "I shall go home and tell my mother, indeed I shall tell everyone, that it was all a misunderstanding, that we never intended to be betrothed."

Penelope shook his arm. "You didn't hear me," she said impatiently. "I said that I want us to pretend we're betrothed."

He looked down at her and smiled sadly. "No, you don't," he said. "I was an unfeeling fool ever to suggest such a thing. I shall take you home now and you shan't ever have to see me again. It would be too much of me to be seen on your doorstep after this. I shall be very sad for it, of course, for I have very much enjoyed your company, but there it is. I have been a fool and I must pay the price."

Not see him again? Penelope felt oddly bereft at the thought. Even if she hadn't come to see the advantages of a pretend betrothal, she would have redoubled her efforts to make Mr. Talbot change his mind just so that she could know she would see him again.

"Please, drive around the park once more," she pleaded.

He hesitated, then agreed. "I confess," he said with a lop-sided smile that tore at her heart, "if this is to be our last drive, I cannot bear to have it end so soon."

"But it need not be our last drive," Penelope said persuasively.

"But surely it must," he replied with a bewildered air.

Penelope shook her head now and bent herself to the task of persuading him to change his mind, once again, about the betrothal.

"You have made me see," she said, "all sorts of advantages to a pretend betrothal between us. No, hear me out before you object. You say you cannot do it because it will hurt my reputation. But do you not see? That is precisely why I like the notion. My parents will never accept that I do not wish to marry. They will bring me out every Season until I am so old that even they must admit my chances are over. And I cannot bear the thought."

"But, don't you ever want to be married?" Mr. Talbot asked, with a puzzled expression. "I know you are not dangling for a husband now, but perhaps in the future your sentiments might change. Eventually you might wish for someone to take care of you."

Penelope snorted rudely. "Take care of me? Make me his prisoner, more likely. I should lose all rights to myself and my property. Whomever I married would have the right to tell me what to do. It is not to be borne! I will not have it. I, and I alone, shall say what is right or wrong for me. I will never give any man the right to do so."

"Yes, but," Mr. Talbot said meekly, "perhaps you could find someone who would not want to tell you what to do. And as a married woman you would have far more freedom than you do now."

Penelope shook her head. "I might. But more likely I would end up with a man who merely pretended he would not tell me what to do and after we were married I would find out otherwise."

"But what if you fall in love?" Mr. Talbot persisted.

Penelope went very pale. "That would be even worse," she said in a voice scarcely above a whisper. "Then I would hand over my rights willingly. I know. I have seen my sisters do just that. They think they are happy, but they are not the same women they were before they married. And I will not allow such a thing to happen to me."

Mr. Talbot looked as if there were something he wished to say but, if so, he did not. Instead, he seemed deep in thought. Finally, he said slowly and cautiously, "You seem to know your own mind very well, Lady Penelope."

"I do. That is why, if you will agree to pretend to be betrothed to me, which would be to both our advantages, you need not fear I would later change my mind."

He seemed unconvinced and Penelope added, "Just think, Mr. Talbot! If we carried out your notion, then every scheming mama in London would hide her daughters from you for fear that you would become betrothed and cry off and ruin her. You would never need to fear matchmaking again, either!"

He hesitated then turned to her. "I will do it," he said reluctantly, "for your sake. I only hope that I am not doing you the greatest disservice in the world."

Penelope squeezed his arm reassuringly. "You are not," she promised him. "I swear you are not. Come, let us go home and tell my parents. I cannot wait to see the stunned look in their eyes!"

Chapter 6

Stunned look was an understatement. The Earl of Westcott and his wife stared at Penelope and Mr. Talbot with
open mouths. Lady Brisbane dropped into a chair and kept
murmuring, "I don't believe it."

Penelope clung to Mr. Talbot for support and he was
more than happy to give it to her. She felt, she realized,
oddly secure as she stood beside him, her hand still clasped
in his, his other arm around her back. A shocking pose, to
be sure, but a secure and reassuring one, and one Penelope
could not bring herself to leave.

Miss Tibbles had been called down to hear the news and
she stared piercingly at her charge, but Penelope made herself smile. It was, perhaps a weak smile, but it was a smile
all the same. And she allowed herself to lean even closer to
Mr. Talbot, her gloved hand resting on his arm. Let them
all believe it was a love match, one that had overborne all
her previous efforts to resist marriage. Then they might not
ask too many questions.

Lord Westcott was the first to recover himself. He
stepped forward and held out his hand. When Mr. Talbot let
go of Penelope's hand to take Lord Westcott's, the earl
shook it vigorously.

"Well, well, I am delighted, simply delighted! Of course
you should have come to me first, but that is neither here nor
there. Of course I approve. I am delighted, simply delighted."

Gradually the color returned to Lady Westcott's face and
she turned to her sister, a smile trembling in place. "We

must begin to plan the wedding, Ariana," she said, hope and joy beginning to fill her voice.

Penelope shifted uncomfortably, a move that did not escape Miss Tibbles's sharp eyes. "I don't suppose," the governess said dryly, "that the pair of you have yet chosen a day for the wedding?"

Penelope colored at the question and she could feel Mr. Talbot doing so as well. She tried to answer and so did he.

"No."

"Not yet."

"That is, we thought it wise to take a few months to become better acquainted first."

"I am waiting for news of an aunt who would wish to come."

"Yes, that's it. Mr. Talbot's aunt. We must wait for news from her."

"Mmm," was all that Miss Tibbles said.

"Aunt?" Lord Westcott snorted. "Nonsense! If she comes, she comes, if not, well, a pity, but that's not a reason for delay."

Lady Westcott, a trifle shrewder than her husband, said hastily, "Oh, but my dear, you must make allowances! I think it charming that Mr. Talbot is so considerate of his aunt. Be pleased, Penelope, for it means he is likely to be considerate of you as well. Of course we will wait for you to have news of your aunt, Mr. Talbot. There is no hurry. And of course it is an excellent notion for the both of you to have time to become better acquainted."

Penelope felt a profound sense of relief sweep over her. They had accepted the story. And the need to postpone the wedding. Now they would leave her alone. At least for a little while.

She looked up at Mr. Talbot and he smiled, kindly, warmly, with the intelligence and understanding in his eyes that she had come to know and like so well.

"I shall take my leave now," he said. "But you may send

for me at any time, if you feel the need," he added softly, in a voice her parents would not be able to overhear.

Then one more squeeze of her hand and Mr. Talbot bowed and took his leave of her family. He really was such a very nice man! The moment he was gone, Penelope took the chance to escape upstairs. Behind her, the moment she, and of course Mr. Talbot, were gone, she could hear voices rise as her family discussed the situation.

Let them, Penelope thought grimly. They would never guess the scheme she and Mr. Talbot had hatched between them. A scheme that would never have been necessary if they both did not have such importunate families!

In the drawing room, no one quite knew what to think. And because they did not, they began to attack one another.

"How could you let him get away with such nonsense, Delwinia?"

"Me? How could you be so ham-fisted as to try to pin him down before a notice has been placed in the papers? What if he panicked and backed out? Better to press him for a date after the betrothal is made public."

"Don't any of you think it odd?"

"No, Ariana!" two voices said as one.

"Penelope is a charming girl. Of course he wishes to marry her," Lady Westcott added with a sniff.

"Oh, of course," Lady Brisbane agreed dryly. "I was thinking more of Penelope's agreement to this. Don't you think that odd, Miss Tibbles?"

The governess eyed them all and merely said in her quiet voice, "I think there is plenty of time to understand it all before the wedding takes place."

And then, before they could ask her what she meant, if, indeed, she meant anything at all, Miss Tibbles excused herself and left the room. She would have gone after Penelope had she been able to think of anything intelligent to ask.

Or been willing to risk that something she said might cause Penelope to call the whole thing off. It was a risk Miss Tibbles was most definitely not willing to take. She had her own suspicions about this betrothal, but even she was too grateful to wish to do anything that might destroy what was, at the very least, a pleasant illusion.

Geoffrey Talbot hummed to himself as he drove home, where he turned his cattle and curricle over to his groom. He was still humming as he mounted the steps and went in search of his mother. He was even still humming as he entered the drawing room and announced grandly, "Mama, Lady Penelope and I are betrothed!"

Silence. Profound, aghast, stunned silence greeted this pronouncement. Four pairs of eyes stared at Talbot. In midstep he halted, choked, and reached automatically to loosen his neck cloth which was suddenly, unaccountably too tight. But he stopped his hand before it reached his neck, and fought down the urge to flee.

"Do come in, dear Geoffrey," his mother said in acid tones. "I am not quite certain that all these ladies heard you."

"Oh, we did, we did!"

"Lady Penelope? The Earl of Westcott's daughter?"

"Impossible! Isn't it?"

"Do sit down, Mr. Talbot, and pray tell us all the glorious details!"

This last was said breathlessly. Geoffrey could not help himself. This time he did turn tail and flee the room. It was not well done of him but he was certain, absolutely certain, that if he stayed he would make matters far worse. He didn't know how, he only knew that his mother's friends would pry out of him details he was quite certain the Westcotts, and Penelope, would prefer to tell their friends themselves. So he turned tail and fled the room.

Sometime later his mother ran him to ground in the small

parlor where he was hiding out, ensconced in a tall chair with the back to the door.

"Coward!" she said, advancing upon the chair, a merciless gleam in her eyes. "How dare you leave me alone, with the worst tattle-mongers in London, after dropping only the titillating tidbit that you and Lady Penelope were betrothed. I hope, for your sake, that it is true. Otherwise we may find Lord Westcott on our doorstep either demanding that you make good on it or else calling you out!"

Now Geoffrey did tug at his cravat. "It is true, Mama," he said.

"And have you set a day for the wedding?" his mother asked with deceptive calm.

"No! That is to say, I don't wish to rush the girl," Geoffrey told her.

Lady Talbot lifted one elegant eyebrow. "You don't?" she asked coolly. "How odd. I thought that was precisely what you wished to do."

"Well, yes, but not to the point she is likely to bolt," he countered with a frown.

Lady Talbot sighed and rolled her eyes upward. "Heaven preserve me from my fool of a son. And you think this will not?" she demanded.

"I didn't know you had company," Geoffrey said defensively. "It was, after all, rather late for anyone to be calling. I assumed you would be alone. You usually are, at this time of the day."

"He assumed I would be alone," Lady Talbot murmured to herself. "How very much like a man!"

Then, more loudly, to Geoffrey she said, "I should advise you, my dear son, not to make such assumptions about Penelope, once you are married. For one thing, she will not like it and for another you are quite likely to be wrong, on some very important matters, and then you will be in the suds. Just as you were today."

Geoffrey stared mutinously at his mother. Still, she had a point. He had never courted a woman before and perhaps he ought to ask her advice about how best to do so.

As though she could read his mind, Lady Talbot nodded, sat down, and said coolly, "Quite right. You do need my advice. The first point of which is to always ask Lady Penelope what she wishes and never to assume that you already know. The second is to listen to her opinions and consider them as thoroughly as you would your own. The third—"

"But Lady Penelope is a woman!" Geoffrey said, aghast.

"Well, of course she is or you would not wish to marry her," Lady Talbot said tartly.

"But it is her duty to listen to my opinions and adopt them as her own," Geoffrey persisted.

Lady Talbot tsked. She shook her head slowly. "Oh, dear. You will have problems in your marriage, won't you?" she said mildly.

On the defensive, he muttered mutinously, "I don't see why. You are the one who is being outrageous. Lady Penelope will surely have the sense to understand that it is my opinions which matter. After all, one thing she is known for is that she is intelligent, almost a bluestocking in fact."

Lady Talbot smiled. "Yes. Intelligent. Why, then, do you think she should adopt your opinions rather than her own? Surely you see the contradiction there? Would you expect your friends to adopt your opinions without considering their own? Blindly, simply because you held them?"

"No, but it is not the same!"

Lady Talbot folded her hands in her lap. "How is it different? Or, rather, how do you think Lady Penelope will think it is different? Oh, I do not doubt that Lady Penelope knows she is supposed to adopt all of her husband's sentiments. Indeed, I suspect that is one of the reasons she is so set against getting married at all. If you expect it of her then perhaps you had best cry off at once. Otherwise I can see nothing but misery for the both of you."

When Geoffrey gaped at his mother, too stunned to speak, Lady Talbot gave a small nod of satisfaction then rose to her feet.

"Think about it," she ordered. "And then ask yourself whether you would have even considered pursuing Lady Penelope if she was the meek creature you have just described. You have said yourself you wish to expose her to new ideas and new ways to think of things. Well, you shall have to choose whether you wish to have an intelligent, independent woman for a wife or whether you wish her to blindly listen to you. You cannot have both."

And with that triumphant pronouncement, Lady Talbot left the room.

Alone, Geoffrey did indeed think about what his mother had said. He wished Lady Penelope to learn and do unusual things, but he had always pictured her doing so under his tutelage. This new image his mother had painted, of her thinking for herself and disagreeing with him, was a most disconcerting one.

And yet, he had the lowering sensation that his mother might very well be right. Suddenly he felt as though he had gotten himself into something far more complicated than he first realized. It was a very humbling experience and Talbot was not accustomed to humility. He did not like the sensation very much. Indeed, he did not, he found, like it at all.

Chapter 7

Geoffrey Talbot was still thinking about what his mother had said the next day when he went to call upon Lady Penelope. Now that they were engaged, he was permitted to take a turn about the garden with her under the watchful eye of her governess, Miss Tibbles. Although she eyed him cautiously, the woman did not intrude. She sat herself on a bench near the house and waved them on to walk to the far, admittedly not very far, corner of the garden if they so chose.

Penelope was as pretty as ever. And he found himself as drawn to her as ever. But Geoffrey still found that it rankled to believe she might take positions different than his own. Like an aching tooth, he could not help but probe the possibility. He still hoped his mother might be wrong, that Lady Penelope would have the good sense to defer to him.

"Tell me, Lady Penelope, what do you think of the situation with the colonies in America?" he asked.

"Former colonies," she corrected him gently.

He wished she would ask his opinion. He wished she would listen and then, if she felt she must, hesitantly advance her own. But she did not. Instead Lady Penelope instantly plunged in with a discussion of her own thoughts.

"I have talked of this with my sister's husband, Lord Winsborough, for he is from the former colonies, you know. And while I do not entirely agree with his point of view, I do believe England has made some errors in judgment."

And then Lady Penelope went on to explain precisely what she thought they were. She talked for some minutes. Only then did she look up at Geoffrey and ask, "What do you think of the situation, Mr. Talbot?"

Mr. Talbot was too annoyed to be able to answer at once. When he did not, she had the audacity to pat his arm and say, very kindly of course, "Never mind. Not everyone takes such an interest in these things as I do."

Now Geoffrey gaped speechless at her, wanting to throttle both Lady Penelope and his mother for giving him the notion to test her theories in the first place.

Finally he managed to say austerely, "I did not say that I had no opinions. I simply choose to think over my answers very carefully before I speak."

She flushed and tilted up her chin. "Quite wise," she said with chill approval. "I, of course, think out my answers well ahead. But please, I am all agog with interest to hear what you will say about the former colonies."

Geoffrey closed his eyes then opened them. He might be inexperienced with the ladies, but even he knew that he had made a fatal error and had best begin with an apology. He tried.

"I meant no disrespect," he said, trying to look sincere. "I merely meant your words gave me much to think about and perhaps I might wish to reconsider my own position in light of some of the things you said."

"Truly? Oh, Mr. Talbot, I do like you!" Lady Penelope said with a smile that dazzled him.

Geoffrey started to feel as if he had managed things very well. But then she added, "What was your position and how have you reconsidered it?"

It really was ridiculously complicated, dealing with ladies, Geoffrey told himself sourly. Now he would have to think of something Lady Penelope had said that he could agree with. And it went very much against the grain to do so even though, he acknowledged with a sigh, he did agree with a number of her points. Though not, he hastily assured himself, with all of them.

Had it been possible, Geoffrey would have mopped his brow, but such a gesture would surely have given him away. Instead he offered Lady Penelope his arm and they began to walk again. He kept his steps as measured as his tones.

She did not seem to mind that he disagreed with some of what she had said. It seemed to be enough for her that he had considered her opinions and argued rationally rather than merely dismissing them out of hand.

By the time their footsteps took the pair back to Miss Tibbles, Geoffrey was beginning to think that he had the hang of this courtship business after all. And that he had been right to think that marriage to an intelligent woman would be preferable to any other sort.

Lady Penelope was smiling up at him in patent approval and even Miss Tibbles had relaxed some of her stare. Surely his mother was wrong to worry, he thought. And there was a distinct lightness in his step as they approached the garden bench where the governess was sitting.

Penelope felt a curious lightness. Mr. Talbot had listened to her! He was the first gentleman she had ever met who was willing to do so. For a moment, a very short moment, she found herself thinking that it was a pity he was not a real suitor.

But then she shook herself. She would not give way to such weakness. It was several years since Penelope had made her vow never to marry, and she was not about to renege on it now. No, if she married she would give up the few rights she had. And that she was not about to do. Not even for a gentleman as nice as Mr. Talbot.

Miss Tibbles was eyeing both of them, Penelope realized, with a speculative gleam in her eyes. Hastily, she tried to divert her governess.

"What is that you are knitting, Miss Tibbles? It looks so very tiny."

"It is for your sister Barbara. Lady Farrington," Miss Tibbles explained to Mr. Talbot.

Penelope snorted in a way that left no doubt as to her disapproval. "I do not see why Barbara had to go and do something so foolish as to get herself with child! Now she cannot do half the things she likes."

Mr. Talbot's lips twitched in something suspiciously like a smile, but his voice was grave as he said, "I suspect, quite strongly, that Lady Farrington did not manage it quite all by herself. As for why, well, perhaps she and Lord Farrington were thinking of something else at the time."

"Mr. Talbot!" Miss Tibbles remonstrated in shocked tones.

Penelope started to protest her governess's impertinence, but Mr. Talbot was not in the least disconcerted. His eyes all but danced with patent amusement as he said to the governess, "What is wrong, Miss Tibbles? Surely you are not trying to tell me that Lady Penelope has the slightest notion of what I am saying?"

There was steel beneath the amusement in his voice and it was Miss Tibbles's turn to be flustered. Penelope watched, fascinated, as her governess tried to find just the right words to answer him.

"I—that is—of course not, but still! I must ask you to be more discreet, sir!"

Miss Tibbles drew herself up to her full diminutive height as she concluded this statement and Mr. Talbot meekly apologized. Too meekly, Penelope realized. His voice did not match the look in his eyes and she stored away the information that Mr. Talbot was capable of dissembling.

As yet it did not occur to her to wonder if, or how, Mr. Talbot might have dissembled with her!

Still, Miss Tibbles seemed to have a sort of instinct about guile, and Penelope decided it would be best to draw Mr. Talbot away from her.

"Let us go inside," she said. "Mama and Aunt Ariana will be wondering where we have gone to."

Mr. Talbot seemed most agreeable to that suggestion. Just as he was agreeable when he made the suggestion that the whole family should join him at Vauxhall Gardens for an evening party. The day and time were set and he quite properly took his leave.

Penelope would not admit, even to herself, that his going left a gap. It was only, she told herself, that she was accustomed to having the house full of callers. But since word had gotten out that she and Mr. Talbot were betrothed, the house was all but empty of callers in the afternoons. No more gentlemen wishing to fix their interest with her, no mothers of daughters calling to assess the competition.

Only the gossipmongers were left. They still came. But instead of watching to see who might prevail, they stared at her avidly, as if by doing so they could fathom what had changed the mind of the wild beauty who was known to have sworn never to marry.

Penelope could not bear it and fled to the sanctuary of her room. There, oddly enough, her thoughts kept returning to Mr. Talbot. But only, she assured herself, because he was the most entertaining person of her acquaintance.

For all her vaunted devotion to honesty, Lady Penelope was, it seemed, capable of a high level of self-deceit.

That evening, at Almack's, matters were even worse. Fingers were pointed. Smiles and titters hidden behind fans. Gentlemen whom Penelope had come to consider part of her court, deserted her for young ladies not yet betrothed.

And while she most certainly did not want the attentions of these young men, still, she found it rankled to see them bowing and smiling and flattering someone else. Only Geoffrey was left to her. And he seemed rather too pleased with himself for her comfort.

As though he understood, he said suddenly, "To the devil with all of them! You need not consider what they say and I am persuaded you are too intelligent to do so. Come, dance with me, and put a smile upon your face. Never let anyone think they have disconcerted you."

Penelope did smile, then, but she shook her head. "I don't wish to dance. I never have. I come only because Mama and Papa and Aunt Ariana insist that I do so."

He was all sympathy. "Where would you choose to be, if you could choose?"

Penelope sighed. Deeply. She didn't even know she did so. Her voice caught at the back of her throat as she spoke aloud the thoughts that had been with her for so long.

"I should like to go to salons. Literary salons, I mean. Scientific salons. Places where people speak their minds and use their minds, yes, and ask all the questions I would, if I could. Salons where one is judged not by how well one knows the steps of a country dance, but rather how well one can think. That is where I would rather be," she concluded defiantly.

But she might have known she needn't be defiant with him. He was looking down at her with patent admiration, and what seemed to be approval, in his eyes. "It is settled, then," he said briskly. "I shall arrange to take you to a salon. No, a series of salons. It may take me a day or two to arrange the invitations, but I have no doubt it can be done."

Then, before she could either object or thank him, he was gone from her side. She watched as he sought out a number of people and she wished fervently that she could hear what he had to say.

She had not even had time to warn him that invitations to a salon were the least of his concerns. He would still need to persuade Mama and Papa to let her go. And that, she thought gloomily, was likely to be more than even his considerable charm could accomplish.

But in this she wronged him. He seemed to know just the things to say to her mother and father and aunt, a short time later.

"The company of the best. A chance for Lady Penelope to widen her circle of acquaintances, here in London. Mutual interests. A good thing to cultivate, prior to marriage, don't you agree, Lady Brisbane?"

Mr. Talbot could not have chosen wiser, Penelope thought as she suppressed a smile. Aunt Ariana prided herself on being an intelligent woman and having been friends with, as well as the wife of, Lord Brisbane.

"Well, perhaps you are right, Mr. Talbot. Delwinia, I do not think it could hurt to let him take her to a salon or two. And I should be willing to accompany them as chaperone."

"Oh, my mother will be happy to do so," he intervened hastily.

"Even better." Lady Brisbane beamed. "Penelope will have a chance to get to know her future mama."

"I suppose it could do no harm," Lady Westcott agreed cautiously.

"Stap me if I don't think he's a right 'un," Lord Westcott said, suddenly making up his mind. "A salon of that sort will suit our little Penelope right down to the ground, I daresay. Eh, puss?"

Penelope objected both to being called little and puss, but she was too shrewd to say so at this moment and risk losing her father's approval. Not when it seemed she would finally achieve her goal. Instead she smiled and said dutifully, "Yes, Papa. It would."

"Good, good, then it's all settled," Lord Westcott said, rubbing his hands together.

Lady Brisbane and Lady Westcott looked at one another and shrugged. Aside from a certain uneasiness, they really could find no objection to the plan, and anything that promoted a growing closeness between Penelope and the man she had finally chosen to marry could only, they concluded, be a very good thing.

Chapter 8

Geoffrey was delighted to have discovered he was right in thinking he knew what Lady Penelope would like. He wasted no time in arranging invitations to a number of literary and scientific salons in London.

The first happened to be one devoted to science. There was a tiny corner of Talbot's mind that was perversely pleased it would be one in which he felt himself on such firm ground. A salon at which he might be held to have something of an advantage over both his mother and Lady Penelope.

But it was more than that. Geoffrey found himself eager to see old friends from his university days. Friends who had continued to pursue scientific interests, as he had, but who had done so here in London, in the company of others, while he had had to retire to the country, where he could keep an eye on his father.

To be sure, Geoffrey had kept in regular touch by correspondence with others following similar courses of research as his own. But it was not the same as having others to talk to, on a daily basis, of his work, as he had while at the university.

So by the time the day came when they were to go to the salon, it was impossible to say which of them was most eager. Even Lady Talbot, to Geoffrey's surprise, was perfectly willing to attend. She was, he thought, oddly enthusiastic. A circumstance for which he was profoundly grateful, if a trifle uneasy.

He was even more grateful when his mother managed to put Penelope at ease within moments of his handing her into their carriage.

"My dear, you cannot imagine how happy I am that you and Geoffrey wish to go to these salons," she said. "It has been far too long since I have so indulged myself and I am very grateful to the pair of you for presenting me with such a wonderful reason to do so again."

Penelope blinked almost shyly at Lady Talbot, then smiled. "I am very much looking forward to it myself," she confessed.

"And so you should be," Geoffrey's mother assured her. "You will enjoy it above all things."

Indeed, so comfortable were his mother and Penelope with one another, that Geoffrey began to feel a trifle nettled. It was not, precisely, that he wished Lady Penelope and his mother to feel very ill at ease. But it would have been nice if they had shown a wish to cling to him. Just a little. Then he could have demonstrated his knowledge, in a kindly way of course, as he explained things to them.

Instead, Lady Penelope looked at him and said, "I am most grateful to you for choosing a scientific salon, Mr. Talbot."

"You are?"

"Oh, yes! What other man would have given me sufficient credit to believe I would understand such things? But you did. It is one of the things I like so much about you!"

Geoffrey could only mumble something and try to avoid his mother's knowing eyes. Eyes that held far too much amusement and understanding for his comfort.

Things were not going according to plan, he thought irritably. It was like one of his experiments gone awry and he had no notion what might happen next.

It ought to have pleased him, then, when Lady Penelope's delight turned to wide-eyed nervousness as they entered the crowded salon and innumerable penetrating eyes were turned upon them. He ought to have been glad she clung to him, as if for protection, as if she felt the urge to turn and flee. This was what he had wanted, wasn't it?

And yet, he knew just how she felt and his first instincts were to comfort her. For he had felt very much the same when he first went up to Cambridge. He tried to tell himself he ought to let her continue to cling to him. He tried to tell himself he ought to demonstrate his superiority by taking part in the nearest conversation, which concerned something he knew a great deal about.

Instead, he looked down at Lady Penelope and smiled reassuringly. "You will do very well," he said softly, so that no one could overhear.

She looked up gratefully. "This is a thousand times worse than Almack's," she confided, her voice as low as his and coming through clenched teeth.

"Impossible!" he rallied her.

She shook her head and smiled wryly. "You do not understand. There I need only be well dressed and follow the rules. Rules I have been taught since my birth. But here! Here I shall be judged upon the quality of my mind and what if I am found wanting?"

She trembled slightly and once again Geoffrey found himself reassuring her. He dropped a hint in her ear about the newly discovered kaleidoscope some men were discussing. And about the latest plans for steamships, when the subject turned to that direction.

They moved about the tiny but very elegantly appointed drawing room and Geoffrey was conscious of his mother's approving gaze on him. Which made him perversely wish to annoy her. But he could not do so. Not when it would come at the expense of Lady Penelope's comfort.

He took an almost personal delight in her progress as she went from listening to interjecting a comment or two. And they actually listened to her. It surprised Geoffrey almost as much as it did Lady Penelope.

They did not always agree with her. Indeed, one or two of the gentlemen in particular seemed to take great delight in arguing any point offered. But they listened. And that seemed to be enough for her. And while he wished to impress her, Geoffrey found there was a certain satisfaction, and a great deal of delight, in watching her fine mind at work and discovering that her tastes in learning had ranged almost as widely as his.

As the evening progressed, Geoffrey watched Lady Penelope smile more and more. And laugh out loud. He found himself wishing she would smile at him like that and laugh at his jests in just such a way.

And then his attention was drawn by two friends who had suddenly discovered his presence.

"Talbot! You're here, in London! How famous! Tell us, what experiments have you been doing of late?"

Penelope could scarcely remember a time when she had enjoyed herself so thoroughly. And she owed it all to Mr. Talbot. She turned to tell him how pleased she was, and discovered that he was deep in conversation with two gentlemen who were discussing gunpowder and fireworks.

Penelope shuddered at the thought and decided to leave him to his own devices for a little longer. It was not that she did not find the subject interesting in theory, for she did. It was rather the image of Mr. Talbot putting himself in jeopardy by handling such dangerous materials that fretted her. And why it should disturb her so deeply was something she preferred not to consider.

Lady Talbot, however, noticed the direction of her glance and moved to Penelope's side. "I have sometimes thought," she said judiciously, "that if Geoffrey had been able to take orders and remain at the university, he would have been much happier."

"Why didn't he?" Penelope asked.

Lady Talbot lifted both eyebrows. "Geoffrey is the only son, indeed, the only child we have. It is clearly his duty to marry and, in time, take up the reins of the family estates. Besides, his father needed him."

The last few words were spoken so softly that Penelope was not entirely certain she had heard them correctly. Still, it made her thoughtful. And softened her heart even further toward Mr. Talbot. He was not made for the round of useless London society any more than she was. And he had not been able to follow his inclinations any more than anyone would let her follow hers.

It made them kindred spirits. Though she could not say so to Mr. Talbot. He might think her sentiments had begun to undergo a change and be so frightened of it that he would insist on breaking off their mock betrothal at once. And that was something Penelope was not ready to do.

No, she would hug to herself the knowledge that here was someone she could truly speak to and know he would understand. And that was worth more than anything in the world to her.

Lady Talbot seemed to read her thoughts. There was amusement in her voice as she said, "Tread lightly, my child. Geoffrey is not always to be taken at face value. There is much there you have yet to learn about and I am not altogether certain you will like it when you do."

Before Penelope could ask her what she meant, Lady Talbot moved away. Once again she was drawn into the conversation, with no time to ponder over the woman's odd words or wonder what they meant. And if the truth be told, at the moment, Penelope simply didn't care. It was not, after all, as though the betrothal were a real one or that it would matter to her what Mr. Talbot's true nature might be.

Sometime later, a gentle hand on her shoulder startled Penelope and she looked up to see Mr. Talbot smiling down at her.

"It is time to go, I fear," he said gently. "My mother is already waiting by the door."

Penelope hastily rose to her feet and made her good-byes. The smiles and requests for her, for all of them to return, held such a genuine note of welcome that she could not help but feel pleased.

Perhaps that was why she felt such a delicious shiver of pleasure when Mr. Talbot placed her cloak around her shoulders with his own hands. Perhaps that was why her heart missed a beat as he smiled down at her and cupped her chin in his hand as he asked, "Did you have a good time?"

"Oh, yes!"

He smiled even more broadly. "You look like a child who has been offered the whole of a sweet shop to enjoy."

Even his gentle teasing could not disconcert her. "I feel as if I have been," she said. "I do not know how to thank you for bringing me here."

Abruptly his expression turned serious. "It is I," he said gravely, "who should be thanking you for prompting me to come. I had forgotten how much I liked, how much I needed, the company of people like these."

Penelope wanted to ask him why he hadn't sought them out on his own. She wanted to ask him why, if he found such company so important to his comfort, he had buried himself in the country away from the possibility. But his mother's words echoed in her mind and she thought she could see a sadness at the back of his eyes that stayed her from speaking her thoughts aloud.

So now she smiled and touched the back of his hand and said gently, "You said your mother was waiting for us. We should be going now."

That drew him out of his reverie and instantly he was once again the young man she was accustomed to seeing. He helped her into the carriage and settled her beside his mother then took the seat opposite, with his back to the horses.

He joked, he teased, he told amusing stories about the evening. But Penelope was not deceived. Somehow, sometime, someone or something had hurt him. And something had drawn him away from what he loved.

Though they were only to be useful tools for one another, ways to keep their families from importuning them to matches they could not want, Penelope found herself hoping that one day Mr. Talbot would confide in her. That he would trust her enough to tell her what it was that brought the shadows to his eyes.

And if he would not tell her, she would listen and watch and try to discover it for herself. Then, perhaps, she could repay his kindness, at least a little, by helping him ease away whatever pain had set the shadows in his eyes.

Penelope had no notion what she was getting herself into. Neither did Geoffrey Talbot. If he had, he might have been sufficiently alarmed to tell her the truth then and there. But how could he guess how persistent she was going to be? Or just what sort of tales her vivid imagination was going to conjure up to explain the mystery his mother had inadvertently created?

Only Lady Talbot would have been amused had she been able to see what the days ahead were going to bring. She would most certainly have said the pair of them deserved it!

As it was, the three of them were merely reasonably content and took leave of one another amiably. The moment Penelope entered Lady Brisbane's town house, however, the magic of the evening dissolved. Her mother and aunt were clearly waiting to quiz her on the evening, and the only thing for which she could be thankful was that her father had decided to play least in sight.

"You did not betray yourself as a bluestocking, did you?" Lady Westcott asked anxiously.

"Mama, that was the whole point of going there."

"But Mr. Talbot! You must remember that you do not wish him to cry off," Lady Brisbane said reasonably.

Penelope turned to her aunt and said defiantly, "Mr. Talbot likes me as a bluestocking."

Both ladies rolled their eyes. "A gentleman may say so, if he wishes to please you," Lady Brisbane said with great patience, "but ten to one he does not really mean it."

"Mr. Talbot does. He doesn't want a stupid wife. My mind is precisely the reason he made his proposal!"

The moment she said those words, Penelope knew they were true. Absolutely true. That if Mr. Talbot ever did marry, he would want someone as intelligent, as well-read, as she was. And suddenly Penelope felt terribly uneasy.

Why didn't Mr. Talbot want to marry her? She was precisely what he would look for in a wife. And he had been willing enough to approach her with his outrageous proposal. He knew she would never importune him with unwanted affections so why had he only wished the betrothal to be a sham?

Unfortunately or, perhaps, fortunately, there was no time for Penelope to dwell on the matter. Her aunt and mother were intent on extracting every detail of the evening from her. They wished to know who she had seen and what everyone had been wearing. They wished to know how the salons had been decorated and even what refreshments had been served.

It was late when Penelope finally escaped to her room for the night and the niggling doubts about Mr. Talbot had long since been thrust to the back of her mind.

Or so she thought. He haunted her dreams all night long, alternating between thrusting her away from him, saying he had no wish for such an antidote to be his wife, and holding her far too close for propriety and whispering that he had plans for her that she had not yet even begun to guess.

Penelope woke in a sweat from each dream and, had she been asked, she could not have said which part disturbed her more. She only knew that she was grateful when morning finally came. How she wished Rebecca were still here!

They were not identical twins, she and Rebecca, but Penelope could not imagine they would have felt closer had they been. And for all the years they were growing up together, they had always talked over everything together.

But Rebecca was married and in the north of England with her husband, Mr. Rowland. Penelope would have to sort matters out alone. All she needed, she told herself, was to see Mr. Talbot again and then she would be able to reassure herself that he was neither an ogre nor an overeager suitor. That he was just her friend.

Or so she told herself.

Chapter 9

But Penelope did not have to sort out matters entirely alone. Morning brought a visit from her older sister, Annabelle.

Penelope would not have been surprised if it had been Rebecca who came to see her. She would not even have been surprised had it been Barbara, the most rebellious of her sisters, for she always took part in whatever mischief was in hand. And Diana might have chosen to meddle, for she had a rebellious streak of her own. But Annabelle? The mildest, most demure, and obedient of her sisters?

Well, perhaps she had come to congratulate her. Still, Penelope was surprised when Annabelle swept into her bedroom and threw her arms around her. "Dearest, we just heard the news and I had to come to London and see you!"

Penelope hugged her sister and then stepped back, aghast, "You have not traveled so soon after the baby was born? Are you all right? Did Winsborough come with you? Is the baby here? How are you? Oh, Annabelle, it is so good to see you again!"

And then, to her great consternation, she burst into tears. Annabelle, however, seemed to understand perfectly. She sat on the edge of Penelope's bed and began to answer the questions quite matter-of-factly.

"I am fine. And yes, Winsborough brought me to London. The baby is also fine and with us. In fact, she is downstairs this very moment, being fussed over outrageously by

Mama and Aunt Ariana, and even Papa and Miss Tibbles are making ridiculous faces at the poor thing."

That drew a gurgle of laughter from Penelope. After a moment, however, Annabelle grew serious again.

"I had to come, Penelope, and speak to you about this betrothal. Are you absolutely certain this betrothal is what you wish?" Annabelle asked.

Taken aback, Penelope said, "I— Of course this is what I wish."

Annabelle peered closer. "Are you certain? If you are not, you could come and stay with us while you decide whether or not to cry off."

Penelope pulled her hands free and rose to her feet. "Why are you saying this to me?" she asked, her concern for her sister patent in her voice. "Are you unhappy in your marriage? Do you regret your choice?"

Annabelle colored rosily. But she met Penelope's eyes with a steady gaze. "I do not regret this marriage. But my first was a mistake. You cannot know how often I have asked myself how I could be so mistaken in a man. Or how I could have allowed Diana to agree to marry a man she had never met just so that it could be my turn."

"Diana is very happy now," Penelope pointed out.

Annabelle nodded. "Yes, the Duke of Berenford turned out to be just the man for her, but I did not know it would be so. None of us did. And all so that I could marry my first Winsborough. Penelope, I came to make certain you were not rushing into anything—that you were not repeating a mistake like mine! Marriage can be a wondrous thing, but it can also be very, very horrid."

Her words came in a rush and she had gone pale. Penelope wanted nothing more than to reassure her. She tried.

"I chose to become betrothed to Mr. Talbot," she said slowly, firmly, "and I shall not hesitate to cry off, if I so choose. You ought to know me well enough to know that," she added with a tiny smile.

"Do you mean to do so?" Annabelle asked, her eyes wide.

Penelope looked away. "I have not yet decided," she said, and was astonished to realize it was true.

Before she could consider the implications of this, Annabelle sighed mistily and smiled. "I was afraid Mama and Papa had forced you to the match, though they both assured me they had not. Oh, Penelope, I have prayed that you might find someone to love, just as I found the second Winsborough!"

That hurt. Penelope had not expected it to do so. After all, had she not decided, long ago, that she never wanted to find someone to love? So why should she regret the reality now? It was not as if she wanted a true betrothal with any man, so why should she find herself wishing that Mr. Talbot looked at her with a tenth of the warmth she had seen the current Lord Winsborough regarding Annabelle?

And how could she let herself think this way? Penelope had promised herself, and Mr. Talbot, that she would only pretend to be betrothed. She had promised that the moment either of them wished to be released from this pretend betrothal she would cry off. How could she, even for a moment, contemplate doing otherwise?

"Penelope? Is something wrong?" her sister asked anxiously.

Before she could answer, before she was forced to answer, Penelope heard footsteps on the stairs.

"Someone must be coming to fetch us," she said brightly. "Come, let us go downstairs together!"

Annabelle rose to her feet, one eyebrow quirked upward. But at least she did not disagree. Still, Penelope thought she heard her sister mutter softly, "I wish I could meet this Mr. Talbot for myself."

Annabelle got her wish that afternoon. And Penelope got, as she thought, the answer to her own doubts and questions. She couldn't have said when the notion first came to her. Or why. But more than a hint of it showed when she and Annabelle went for a walk in the park that afternoon. Her older sister seemed so young and full of laughter that Penelope found herself laughing as well. And there they met Mr. Talbot. He was walking with his friend, Reggie Hawthorne.

The two men were walking quite closely together, and laughing as well, though in their case at some rude jest, no doubt. They made a handsome pair, Mr. Talbot with his burnished dark blond hair and Mr. Hawthorne with his red curls. Mr. Hawthorne was the first to notice the ladies and raised his quizzing glass to stare at them.

"I say," Penelope could hear him tell Mr. Talbot, "ain't that your fiancée? And someone with her."

The instant he saw her, Mr. Talbot's face seemed transformed. He smiled and hurried forward, pulling his friend with him. "Lady Penelope! How delightful to see you. And who is this lovely lady? I have not had the pleasure of her acquaintance."

"This is my sister, Annabelle. Lady Winsborough, I should say," Penelope hastened to explain. "And Annabelle, this is Mr. Talbot and his friend, Mr. Hawthorne."

"How de do," Mr. Hawthorne said, bowing low.

His voice was polite enough, but his attention immediately began to wander. "There's another!" he told Mr. Talbot.

Both ladies looked but could not imagine what Mr. Hawthorne was pointing at. Mr. Talbot took pity on them. "We have a wager, Reggie and I, as to how many dogs we shall see riding in the park this afternoon."

"Dogs?" Annabelle said faintly.

"Yes, dogs. Damnedest fashion I've ever seen, and so I've told Geoffrey. Oh, beg pardon," Hawthorne said, realizing they were frowning at him disapprovingly. "Forgot myself. Not fit company for ladies, you know. Don't seek it. Don't wish it. Wouldn't tolerate it but for m'family. In-sist I go. Think I'll get married one of these days. I won't, but there's no telling them so. Especially with Talbot here getting himself betrothed. M'family says that if he could get betrothed, anyone could, and I ought to do likewise."

Abruptly Talbot trod heavily on his friend's foot, not even bothering to hide the gesture. Hawthorne hastily shut up. But not before a speculative gleam appeared in Annabelle's eyes.

Penelope, meanwhile, wished there was a way to reas-sure Mr. Hawthorne that his friend wasn't really betrothed. But then she realized that she couldn't very well do so without giving everything away, even if Annabelle had not been at her side. For Mr. Hawthorne was clearly the sort of sad rattle who would tell anything to anyone before realiz-ing that he ought not to do so. She held her tongue.

"Will you accompany us a little way?" Annabelle asked Mr. Talbot in dulcet tones that in any of her other sisters would have meant mischief.

In fact, Penelope was not so certain it did not. Before she could warn him off, Mr. Talbot agreed and offered Penelope his arm. Mr. Hawthorne, with good grace, perhaps because he knew Annabelle was already married and therefore could pose no threat to his own unwed state, fell into step with her.

"You are looking well today," Mr. Talbot said stiffly, as though conscious of her sister's eyes boring into his back.

"Thank you," Penelope answered just as stiffly.

She was not, whatever Annabelle might hope or think, going to give her sister the satisfaction of overhearing any-thing of interest.

Annabelle, however, had other notions. In her sweet way she asked, "Mr. Hawthorne, tell me, have you and Mr. Tal-bot been friends long?"

"Oh, for years," Hawthorne answered affably. "Made friends at the university. Liked it there. We both did. Would have been happy never to leave. Families wouldn't let us stay. Thought we ought to take our place in the *ton*. Heirs, you know."

Penelope could feel Mr. Talbot grow tense beside her. She tried to reassure him. "It is quite all right," she said gently. "I have friends and relatives who put me to the blush as well, you know."

He gave her a grateful look. But Penelope's attention was caught by Hawthorne's next few words.

"Course Talbot and I ain't much for doing the pretty. Much rather be in the company of other fellows."

He added something else, but Penelope couldn't hear what it was. Or her sister's reply. Mr. Talbot's hand over hers was much too disconcerting. She felt herself blush in earnest and began to speak, rushing her words.

"I must apologize for my sister. She is not usually such a shocking gossip. I don't know what has come over her. I—"

A finger over her lips startled Penelope into sudden silence. She looked up to discover Mr. Talbot looking at her with patent amusement on his face. And something else. Kindness.

"It really is all right," he said.

And to her surprise, Penelope realized she believed him. She was disappointed when he announced, a moment later, that he and Hawthorne must leave them, for they had an appointment and they were already late. There were some questions she wished she could think of a way to ask him.

Penelope watched their departing backs, oblivious to everything else, until Annabelle touched her arm and said gently, "I think it is time that we returned to Aunt Ariana's town house."

They walked back and talked of the two men but Penelope did not share all her own thoughts. She agreed that Mr. Talbot and his friend were amiable. She agreed that Mr. Talbot was a most handsome man. She accepted her sister's kind words almost as a balm. But Penelope shared none of her own growing suspicions. Indeed, she shared them with no one, almost afraid to speak the possibilities aloud.

They reached the town house and Annabelle went into the drawing room to be with her mother and aunt. Penelope sought the quiet of her room instead. There she found Rebecca's cat, one she had rescued but left behind when she married Mr. Rowland, on her bed. Penelope set the cat on her lap and began to stroke its fur to hide the trembling in her hand. Here was someone she could safely talk to!

Solemnly she informed the feline, "I fear I may have solved the mystery as to why Mr. Talbot doesn't wish to marry me!"

The cat regarded her stoically. Penelope glanced to be certain she had closed the bedroom door, then she said, leaning close to the cat's ear, "Uncle Frederick."

The cat blinked and began to lick a paw. "Yes," Penelope said with a decisive nod. "Uncle Frederick. He has never wished to marry, either."

She stroked the cat and was silent for some moments, her fertile mind working rapidly. "It explains so much," she said at last. "No wonder Lady Talbot is trying so hard to force his hand. Just like Mama and Papa, she must think it a disgrace if he does not marry. Mind you, I think Uncle Frederick is wonderful for standing by his principles. Why should he marry when he is certain he would make himself and any woman miserable by doing so? And just like Uncle Frederick, Mr. Talbot must be determined not to make such a horrendous mistake."

The cat meowed. Penelope answered her quite seriously. "Yes, I know Mama and Papa do not like or approve of Uncle Frederick but he has always been *my* favorite uncle. Why should I not like Mr. Talbot for having the same qualities I admire in him?"

The cat leaped from Penelope's arms. She went over her suspicions once again. Could she be mistaken? Undoubtedly. And yet everything seemed to fit. If only Rebecca were here. It would be so much easier with someone like her sister to talk things over!

But Rebecca was in the north with Mr. Rowland and very busy, it seemed. She could not come. Penelope tried to tell herself there was no need to talk with Rebecca. Nothing truly had changed. Indeed, she ought to feel safer than ever with Mr. Talbot. And she did. What could be better? He was a friend who was kind and understanding and who would never press her to allow undesirable attentions.

A gleam in her eye, Penelope rose to her feet, shook out her skirts, and went downstairs to be with her sister and mother and aunt. And, if the baby were not sleeping, her newest niece.

In a way, it was a relief to finally understand. She had the best of all possible situations, she told herself—a fiancé, but one who would never importune her. Yes, this was all working out marvelously well and the best thing was, no one but herself suspected the truth.

Chapter 10

Upon reflection, Penelope decided that she might very well be wrong. Still, she found herself watching Mr. Talbot and wondering. And she sat down to write her uncle a long letter about the betrothal.

As for Mr. Talbot, Geoffrey was feeling very pleased with himself. He had, after all, accomplished what no one else had done, he had breached the defenses of the Ice Princess. She was, he was certain, beginning to look quite kindly on him. Of course, there was still the question of what she was going to do when she discovered he didn't want to break off their betrothal, but he had sufficient arrogance to think that by the time the question arose, she would be so enamored of his excellent qualities she would forgive him anything.

And he should have been reassured. After all, as the days passed, she was happy to talk to him, to spend time with him, more so than ever before. She enjoyed attending salons in his company, and he even coaxed a laugh out of her on the dance floor at Almack's.

His triumph ought to have been complete. Except that something seemed to be nagging at him. Some quality of her companionship that argued she was comfortable with him but did not precisely look at him as a potential husband.

Had Geoffrey Talbot had sisters, he would have recognized the situation far sooner. He would have known that Lady Penelope was treating him like a favorite brother.

But then again, perhaps it was as well he didn't. It is unlikely it would have had a beneficial effect upon his temper. As it was, the realization, when it came, and in the circumstances it occurred, took him so entirely by surprise that Geoffrey didn't have time to be angry.

They were at Vauxhall Gardens and everything seemed to be going splendidly. Lady Penelope's parents, the Earl of Westcott and his wife, and her aunt, Lady Brisbane, and the Duke and Duchess of Berenford were all present.

Geoffrey had not met Lady Penelope's eldest sister, Diana, before, but he had known Berenford when they were both at Cambridge, though Berenford was a few years older than he. They had become known to one another through the similarities of their academic interests. The friendship had been sealed through certain exploits that both would prefer never came to light.

All should have been well. The food was excellent, the wine flowed freely, and everyone seemed happy. When Lady Penelope agreed to go with Mr. Talbot for a walk along the shadowed lanes, he was certain his plans were in excellent train.

Lady Penelope tucked her hand into the nook of his elbow trustingly enough. And she talked with such ease that a stranger might have been pardoned in thinking they were old friends. It was only when she suddenly stopped, gave a tiny cry of pleasure, and called out to one of London's most beautiful and eccentric young men, that Geoffrey felt a twinge of alarm.

To be sure, he had seen the fellow at one of the salons they had attended, but had kept his distance, knowing something of Manton's reputation. That must be it, he told himself. Surely Lady Penelope had met him there and, too innocent to think anything of it, made friends with the fellow.

Now she was saying, "I must make you known, Mr. Talbot, to Mr. Manton. He is no relation to that shocking fellow who has a shooting gallery. Mr. Manton, I am certain you and Mr. Talbot have a great deal in common."

Both men recoiled, startled at the suggestion. They peered at one another and were not reassured. "Indeed?" Mr. Manton asked doubtfully.

"Oh, yes," Penelope assured him eagerly. "Both of you prefer the company of men to women and both of you are interested in literature."

Mr. Manton stifled what Geoffrey was certain was a snicker. "Oh, yes, so much in common," he agreed. "Do call on me anytime at all, Mr. Talbot."

And then the fellow had the audacity to flutter his lashes at Geoffrey who was more confused than anything else. He had to stop Lady Penelope before she said anything more to embarrass herself or either of them.

"No doubt Mr. Manton and I shall encounter one another again at a salon or two," he said easily. "You are kind to introduce us, Lady Penelope, but we must not keep Mr. Manton from his friends."

There was no malice or anger in Geoffrey's voice and something of the wariness in Mr. Manton's stance eased. He even smiled slightly, a friendly smile this time, and bowed to Lady Penelope as he said, "Mr. Talbot is quite right, I do have friends waiting. A delight to see you, Lady Penelope. To see both of you."

Then, with a slightly bemused look upon his face, Mr. Manton continued on his way. Geoffrey, meanwhile, was hard put to keep a frown off his own face. He steered Lady Penelope toward a more deserted path, hoping that no one would overhear her artless comments.

"Didn't you like Mr. Manton? I was certain the two of you would get along well," she said.

"And why would you think that?" Geoffrey asked, genuinely curious to hear her answer.

"Why because the both of you are like my Uncle Frederick," she said innocently. "You both prefer the company of

men to that of women. I thought you would like being introduced to someone you might not know who felt the
same."

Geoffrey choked. He missed a step. His head swam and
he felt himself turn a deep red. He hastily looked around to
make absolutely certain no one could have overheard Lady
Penelope. That no one could have understood the implications of the encounter between himself and Mr. Manton.

"Where—did—you—get—such—a—notion?" he demanded, trying to keep his own voice low and his temper
under tight control.

"I don't precisely know," Penelope said honestly, "I just
know that at some point I realized how very much you
were like my Uncle Frederick."

Geoffrey, who had heard rumors, said tightly, "I am not
like your Uncle Frederick."

Penelope stopped right where she was on the path and
looked up at him earnestly. "It is quite all right, Mr. Talbot,
I assure you. I shan't give you away. I like my Uncle Frederick. Truly I do. Indeed he is my favorite uncle."

"But I don't—that is to say, I do like women," Geoffrey
said, feeling a trifle desperate.

Lady Penelope made soothing clucking sounds. "There,
there, Mr. Talbot, it is all right. You needn't pretend with
me."

"I—am—not—pretending."

She gave a sigh of exasperation. "Of course you are.
Why else would you have come up with an absurd notion
like this pretend betrothal of ours?"

And then his control snapped. Anyone, he thought,
would be pardoned for doing as he did. He drew Lady Penelope into his arms and thoroughly kissed her. When he
was done, he lifted his head and said, "There. Does that
seem like I don't like women?"

To his utter astonishment, and absolute fury, Lady Penelope chuckled! She actually had the temerity to chuckle at him!

"You are an excellent actor, sir. Why, under other circumstances, you might have made your fortune on the stage. But you cannot fool me. Come, Mr. Talbot, we had best return to my family before they come in search of us. Even though we are supposed to be betrothed, I cannot think they would be pleased to see how you just behaved."

Geoffrey Talbot wished he could drop his head in his hands and howl with disbelief and despair. But there was no time. Lady Penelope was already striding with unladylike haste toward the more well-lighted path, and by the time she reached it he had best be at her side.

He caught up with her and tried to decide how to plead his case. But nothing he could think of would have the slightest effect upon her if his earlier efforts had not.

Geoffrey had started the evening thinking he had matters well in hand and that he would be married by the end of the summer after all. Now he despaired of coming out of this with either his reputation or his self-esteem intact. How the devil could she make a monumental mistake like this?

Nor did it help that when they reached the Westcott party, all eyes immediately turned on them and took in his bemused state and Lady Penelope's air of patent satisfaction. In Berenford's eyes he fancied he even saw a hint of laughter. Laughter Geoffrey was not in the mood to endure just now.

He did not know how he made it through the rest of the evening. Certainly his answers were more disjointed than usual and produced nods of indulgent understanding from Lady Westcott and Lady Brisbane. It only wanted the mincing trill of Mr. Manton's voice to set the seal on it all.

"Oh, Mr. Talbot. Halloo, again. I wanted to tell you what a pleasure it was to be introduced to you tonight. And how I do so look forward to forming a better acquaintance with you!"

And then, before Geoffrey could even begin to think of a suitable reply, the laughing fellow was off to join a party of friends.

It did not help that Lord Westcott cleared his throat and shook his head and said in a fatherly way, "I daresay you haven't a notion, but it would not do to encourage that connection, Mr. Talbot. Mr. Manton has, shall we say, interests that are very different from your own. No need to be embarrassed, m'boy. You couldn't know. A word to the wise, that's all."

Lady Westcott and Lady Brisbane avoided his eyes but still they nodded in agreement. The Duchess of Berenford looked confused but Berenford, damn his eyes, had to cover his mouth to hide his laughter.

Indeed, Berenford managed to find a moment when everyone else in the party was talking to one another. In a low voice that would not carry, he said, "I shan't ask what rig you are running, but it seems a very strange one to me."

"It is not my fault that Lady Penelope has taken some odd notions into her head," Geoffrey retorted bitterly.

"Isn't it?" Berenford asked, his eyebrows rising skeptically. "I should have thought it was precisely your fault. You are not acting like yourself. At least not very like the Talbot I know."

With a careful glance to be certain no one was listening, Geoffrey sketched out his strategy to Berenford. "Hmmm, it might work at that," the duke admitted.

"Do you mean to tell on me?" Geoffrey asked warily.

Berenford looked even more surprised than before. "Me? Why the devil should I do that? I did far worse when I masqueraded as a groom to discover what Lady Diana was like before I married her! No, you are on your own with this. I shall neither aid nor hinder your cause. But be careful. Your reputation will not stand for too much friendship with men like Manton."

Geoffrey damned his eyes but had no time to do more.

Already the others were turning to draw them back into the conversation. But Berenford's words gave him something to think about.

Had he been able to do so, Geoffrey could cheerfully have strangled Lady Penelope. Except that she was looking at him with such wide, soulful eyes, trying so earnestly to reassure him, that all he really wanted to do was hold her in his arms, and fold her against his chest.

How the devil could you be angry with a woman who just wanted to help?

If only there were someone he could talk it over with, but this was not the sort of thing Geoffrey dared share with anyone. His friends would think it too good a jest to keep secret and others might not realize it wasn't true.

If only Lady Penelope hadn't taken such a notion into her head. And if only she hadn't told him or done anything about it. If only she weren't so blasted sure of herself.

Of course, Penelope wasn't nearly as sure of herself as Mr. Talbot thought. Particularly after that kiss on the dark path. And after Diana drew her aside to talk.

"My dear, Berenford has the greatest respect for Mr. Talbot, but I, of all people, know what it is like when Mama and Papa get some notion in their head. And it seemed to me that when you and Mr. Talbot returned from your walk, neither of you looked best pleased. Is everything all right?"

"Of course," Penelope said brightly.

"You know that if you should decide to cry off, we would all stand by you," Diana persisted anxiously.

Penelope did know that. She had known it from the moment she agreed to this outrageous proposal. But how could she tell them she didn't want anyone to stand by her? That she wanted to be considered no longer an eligible *parti* by the *ton*?

Or worse, if Penelope did tell them the truth, how could she also tell them, when she could scarcely acknowledge it to herself, that there were moments when she did not wish to cry off after all? Like tonight, after Mr. Talbot kissed her.

She tried to tell herself it meant nothing. It was an effort to fool her. As Mr. Talbot had fooled everyone else. But it didn't make a particle of difference. Because it wasn't Mr. Talbot she was worried about. It was herself. How could she feel this way about someone who didn't even like women? What was there about her that could want to cling to him and beg for more?

It was a very lowering thought to realize that after guarding her heart so long, from so many gentlemen who wanted her, she found it touched by someone who did not.

But that was something Penelope could scarcely tell Diana. So she answered her eldest sister with a smile and made some sort of jest or two about knowing exactly what she was doing, and then she steered them back over to the rest of the party and made certain no one else had a chance to corner her alone for the rest of the evening.

But her thoughts kept straying to Mr. Talbot and how unexpectedly right it had felt when he held her and kissed her. And then she would have to remind herself that how it felt was quite beside the point. Penelope had made a bargain with Mr. Talbot and it was not his fault she found herself in such a quandary. She would keep her part of the bargain and he need never know she had ever felt such things about him.

She told herself so over and over again. Right up until the moment her maid helped her undress for bed. And even as she did, Penelope could not help gently touching her lips and wondering if Mr. Talbot would ever kiss her again. If her maid wondered at the gesture, she did not say so, and after the girl was gone, Penelope sat by the window and leaned her forehead against the glass.

What was she going to do? Surely it was foolish to repine over the matter? Surely she ought to be happy that if she was going to lose her heart at all, it was to a gentleman who would not, could not want to marry her? This way she need not fear losing herself or her rights.

And yet none of this, no matter how sensible, seemed to help and it was a long time before Penelope sought her bed and even longer before she fell asleep.

Chapter 11

Rebecca was the first person Penelope had written to, knowing her twin would want to hear about the betrothal firsthand. It had not been easy, for Penelope could not tell even her sister the truth and she feared her blithe comments would not serve.

The first letter back from Rebecca merely asked for details. The second more persistently asked the same. Finally she wrote quite bluntly:

> *From what you say in your letters, or rather from what you do not say, Penelope, I am afraid Mama and Papa have forced you to the match. If this is so, come to me and Hugh and I shall give you sanctuary. If this betrothal is what you wish, then I shall be very happy for you, but I cannot help recalling your vow never to marry and find it hard to believe you have changed your mind. Please write and tell me for I shall be in agony until I hear from you.*

Penelope set down the letter with a sigh. It was a very lowering thought that no one seemed to believe she could possibly have entered into this betrothal of her own free will. Although perhaps, she had to admit, she had given them reason to think it unlikely. Particularly Rebecca.

If only she could be sure of her own mind! With a sigh Penelope rose and went to write a reply. Rebecca meant kindly and she did not wish her to worry longer than necessary.

But how, precisely, was she to reassure her sister? She could not, she found, put into writing all the thoughts and doubts that assailed her. Or her suspicions about Mr. Talbot's nature. Or the outrageous bargain she had made with him.

Nor could she lie and tell Rebecca that she was reconciled to marriage after all. In the end, Penelope wrote first to her uncle, telling him more about Mr. Talbot and asking his advice. And whether any woman could have changed his mind about marriage.

She almost crossed out that last, but didn't. After this note was folded and sealed, Penelope scribbled a light and reassuring note to Rebecca and hoped it would be enough to hold her sister where she was. For of all people in the world, Rebecca was the only one she did not think she could fool. And yet, it was a tempting notion to go to her and pour out her hopes and fears. If only Rebecca were not so far away!

Even as she took her letters downstairs to post, Penelope's thoughts kept turning to Mr. Talbot and she wondered what he was doing.

Mr. Talbot was doing his damnedest not to yell at his mother. She was sipping her tea and regarding her son with a very sharp gaze. "Tell me again, Geoffrey, why Mr. Manton conceives himself to be a great friend of yours."

"How the devil did you hear about that?" he demanded. "It only happened last night."

"Do not curse at me," she said tartly. "As for how I know, you should realize by now that mothers know everything. Now tell me about Mr. Manton."

Geoffrey sighed. In truth he was not entirely averse to confiding in her. He would not have volunteered to do so, but since she insisted, he said, choosing his words and tone of voice very carefully, "Lady Penelope thought it would be a kindness to introduce the two of us. Because we have, as she concluded, so many common interests."

For a long moment Lady Talbot stared at her son. Then she gave a tiny shout of laughter.

"I am delighted to afford you so much amusement, Mother," Geoffrey said sardonically.

She laughed again. "Well, it is amusing," she told him. "And you would agree were it anyone but yourself involved in this. So it has come back to haunt you, this pretense of yours that you wish never to marry?"

"It is not entirely pretense," he said. "I have been wary of marriage."

"Frightened to death, more like."

He flushed. His lips tightened into a straight line and a haunted look came into his eyes as he remembered his childhood. "I did not want," he admitted, "to find myself shackled to someone I could not respect. As you did."

It was plain speaking and she set down her teacup with a snap. There was no more laughter in her eyes and indeed there were shadows that mirrored his own.

"I have always been sorry," Lady Talbot said, her voice a trifle unsteady, "that you had to witness what you did. But in recent years things have been much better."

Instinctively he reached out to her, but she waved his hand away. "I am sorry," he said, shaken. "I should not have said what I did."

She rose to her feet and turned her back on him to stare out the window. Over her shoulder she said, "I have tried to shield you from as much as I could. I never wanted my experience to haunt yours."

"But without it, I might have made a fatal marriage years ago," he countered. "Do not be sorry, Mama. I shall do much better because of what I saw."

Now she whirled to face him. Her hands gripped the back of a chair. "Will you?" she demanded. "When your wisdom has brought you to such a pass that you will try to trick an innocent girl into marriage with you? I should intervene if I did not think her intelligent enough to see through you on her own."

Geoffrey rose to his feet, surprisingly calm. He came around the table and took his mother's hands in his own. "It is all right, Mother," he said gently. "I am doing this simply because it is the only way to woo Lady Penelope. And she is the only woman I can imagine wanting to marry because she is the only woman I have ever met who is half as intelligent as you are."

That surprised a watery chuckle from Lady Talbot. "Do not talk nonsense to me!" she snapped.

But still she smiled. And that was enough for Geoffrey. He grinned impishly, and said, "Lady Penelope will lead me a merry dance and you will enjoy every moment of it."

"I only hope she may!" his mother retorted, with something of her old humor back again. "And this business with Mr. Manton is an excellent beginning. You had best hope, however, that no one else takes it seriously."

Fortunately the encounter loomed larger in Geoffrey's mind than in that of anyone else who had seen it. Still, he went through the day half afraid someone was going to speak of it. No one did. Except, of course, Lady Penelope.

"Perhaps Mr. Manton will be in the park today," she said when he came to take her out for a drive.

"I don't wish to see Mr. Manton."

She looked at him, wide eyed. "Oh. You didn't like him then? I only meant to help. I know that my Uncle Frederick was used to say that it could be very hard to others who looked at life as he did."

Geoffrey nearly choked at that. Still, he held his tongue. It was not for him to disillusion her. Except on the subject of needing to find him friends.

"I have no trouble finding others who look at life as I do," he said severely.

"Oh. No doubt it comes of being in the city," she said, considering the matter. "Perhaps I should suggest to Uncle Frederick that he come here."

Not a word. He wouldn't say a word. Not when anything he said might make matters worse. After a moment she nodded. "That is what I shall do. I shall suggest to Uncle Frederick that he should make a visit to London. And then you can meet him. You both have so much in common."

Geoffrey would have closed his eyes save that he was driving his grays and it was all he could do to hold them steady as it was.

"I think," he said carefully, "it would be best if you looked to yourself, rather than to solve the problems of others."

"Myself?"

Her voice seemed to quaver and Geoffrey softened his tone. "What you mean to do, after we cry off our betrothal, of course," he explained.

She hesitated. "I am not entirely certain," she said. "I once thought I would set up household on my own. But now I wonder if that would really do. Perhaps I could travel. But not for years. Mama and Papa would never allow it. I don't really know what I shall do. Probably there will be such a dreadful scandal that Mama and Papa will insist upon taking me home. And I shall languish there, reading and doing my best to learn on my own."

"It sounds a dismal prospect," he said impulsively.

She looked up at him and grinned and he thought her face enchanting beneath the straw bonnet she wore. "It is," she agreed. "Almost as bad as being married."

Here was his opening. But before he could suggest that perhaps they ought to go through with the marriage after all, she settled back and said quite firmly, "But do not fear that I mean to entrap you, Mr. Talbot. I shall hold to our agreement, dismal prospects or not. When we both deem sufficient time to have passed, I shall cry off. I have grown far too fond of you to treat you otherwise."

Now how the devil was he to argue with that? He could only say sourly, "How kind of you, Lady Penelope. And most honorable."

"Do you know," she said reflectively, "I have been raised to value honor highly. I think there are few things I abhor as much as deceit."

Geoffrey felt his cravat growing distinctly tighter. Still, he tried. In as careless and offhand a manner as he could manage, he told Lady Penelope, "Well, if you should change your mind, we are becoming such excellent friends I think you could tell me."

A distinctly unladylike snort of disgust was her only reply. And that, Geoffrey thought gloomily, settled that. He turned the curricle toward Lady Brisbane's town house. Even as Lady Penelope's betrothed, there were limits as to how long he might keep her out and he had already overstepped those bounds more than once.

Indeed, so discouraged was he, that the sight of Lady Penelope's governess, Miss Tibbles, acted almost as a tonic. Particularly when that redoubtable lady stepped forward and greeted them upon their return.

"A word with you, sir," she said as he handed Penelope out of his curricle.

Geoffrey tilted his head quizzically to one side as he tossed the reins to his groom. "Certainly."

Penelope would have stayed and listened but a word from Miss Tibbles sent her inside. Bemused, Geoffrey waited for the governess to tell him what was troubling her.

"I wish to know your intentions, sir," she said, drawing herself up to her full height and looking him directly in the eye.

Geoffrey looked down at her, amused. "Why, I am betrothed to Lady Penelope," he replied. "Surely someone has told you as much. Indeed, I recall you were there when Lady Penelope and I told her family."

"That is not what I mean," Miss Tibbles persisted, beginning to tap one toe impatiently. "When do the pair of you mean to come to the point and set a wedding date?"

A wry smile crossed Geoffrey's face. He was utterly honest as he said, "I should be happy to set a date the moment Lady Penelope is willing to do so. But as yet I think she would only bolt if I tried to press her on the point."

Miss Tibbles's grim expression softened a trifle. She sighed. She looked at him anxiously. "But you are still planning to marry her?"

"Yes."

"Good. She is an excellent young woman, and far more intelligent than most, which I collect is not a disadvantage with you. Still, she is troubling when she becomes stubborn like this. Very well, I shall do what I can to encourage her to come to the point. I only wished to be certain that you still wished it as well."

Now Geoffrey was amused. "And if I were not?" he asked. "Do you mean to say you would encourage her to cry off, despite the scandal it would cause if she did so?"

Miss Tibbles looked at Geoffrey and all the sternness was once again back. "Mr. Talbot," she said frostily, "I should encourage Lady Penelope to do whatever seemed most likely to make her happy, whether that would mean crying off or carrying through with this marriage. She means a great deal to me and though it is probably not my place to say so—"

"It is not," he promptly agreed.

She ignored the interruption. "It is not my place to say so but I tell you frankly that if she marries you and I discover that you have made her unhappy, you will have me to answer to and not just her father and mother!"

Geoffrey bit his lower lip to keep from laughing at the governess quivering with emotion. "Yes, Miss Tibbles," he said meekly. And when she would have opened her mouth to upbraid him further, he said earnestly, "I, too, wish to see Lady Penelope happy. And I believe that her happiness lies with me, as my wife. I swear that I shall never do anything to hurt her, if I can help it."

Miss Tibbles brushed away something that looked suspiciously like a tear or two. She sniffed and said, "Very well, then. That is all I wished to say. Good day, Mr. Talbot."

And then, with her back held ramrod straight, Miss Tibbles marched up the steps and into Lady Brisbane's town house.

Smiling to himself, Geoffrey climbed into his curricle and took the reins back from his groom. Well, he thought, one could not say he was not marrying into an entertaining household! And with that, he set the horses to.

Chapter 12

Frederick Baines read the missive from his niece with something of a frown and something of a smile upon his face. He was delighted that she was fond of, and felt she could confide in him. And her description of this Mr. Talbot sounded quite intriguing. At the same time, he did not at all like the notion that she had gotten herself betrothed to someone who could not love her.

With a thoughtful air, Frederick tapped his chin. He really was fond of Penelope. And her sisters, of course. But Penelope was the one who had need of him now. Perhaps, he decided, it was time for a visit to London. The family would not like it, but that weighed less with him than his concern for his niece.

Rising from his chair, Frederick called for his valet. "Matthew, it is time to pack for a trip to London!" he said.

Penelope stared angrily at her visitor, Lady Pinkwell. Two bright spots of red dotted her cheeks as she said coolly, "Indeed?"

Lady Pinkwell tittered. "Oh, my, yes, Lady Penelope. All of London is agog to see what you will do. I assured them you would never be so foolish as to cry off, and that even if you were, your parents would never be so foolish as to allow it. But people will not listen. You have not set a date and so they are persuaded you will never do so. I do not go so far as those who call both you and Mr. Talbot unnatural, but even I fear you may put yourself beyond the pale with such behavior."

Penelope started to rise to her feet, a thundering rage in her breast, when a lazy voice from the doorway forestalled her.

"Lady Pinkwell. How foolish of you to listen to such nonsense. I am persuaded my fiancée has too much sense to do so."

"Mr. Talbot," Lady Pinkwell said faintly.

He advanced into the room and Penelope watched him in amazement. This was a side of Mr. Talbot she had never seen before. He dealt with Lady Pinkwell utterly ruthlessly.

"Now, were it your poor daughters, one could understand the concern. But you forget, Lady Penelope is the daughter of an earl, with an ample dowry, and she is beautiful into the bargain. I cannot think anything she might do would be sufficient to make her ineligible in the eyes of any sensible gentleman. Or any sensible gentlewoman."

It was a rout, an utter rout. Lady Pinkwell's bosom rose and fell rapidly with patent indignation. Her cheeks colored and she opened her mouth several times to retaliate. Except that she shut it again just as quickly. Then Mr. Talbot administered the coup d'etat.

"A pity you must be going, Lady Pinkwell," he said with a bow. "Pray give my regards to Lord Pinkwell."

There was nothing for the poor lady to do but retreat. Dazed, Penelope stared at Mr. Talbot as though she were seeing him for the first time. Which, in some sense, she felt she was.

He came over and sat down beside her and took her unresisting hand in his. He even kissed her fingertips. "My poor dear," he said gently, "has it been this bad with everyone?"

"I wanted to box her ears," Penelope admitted. "If you had not come, I daresay I should have tried."

"But where is your mother? And aunt? Why is there no one here to defend you against such creatures?"

Penelope sighed. "They went to visit an acquaintance of my aunt. I did not wish to go, fearing just such a quizzing. And then, when Lady Pinkwell came to call I thought it would be a distraction to receive her and her daughters. She has always before, you see, been quite kind to me. Kinder than most. Only this time she came alone and she was not kind at all."

This last was said naively and Mr. Talbot's eyes began to twinkle. "Ah, but that was because your drawing room was always filled with gentlemen and she hoped one or more might transfer their affections from you to her daughters. Now that that hope is gone, she feels no need to restrain her wicked tongue."

Penelope sighed. "A great many people have proved to be the same. I suppose it is just as you say, only I find it so very disillusioning."

"I know," he agreed. "But you have me. Surely that is some consolation."

She looked at him earnestly as she replied, "It is. Only you cannot, will not, be here forever. And then what shall I do?"

Penelope only meant to be honest. She thought she stood upon such terms with Mr. Talbot as made such honesty acceptable, perhaps even preferable to him. Why then was he suddenly looking at her in such a strange way? And why was he bending his head so close to hers?

She was entirely unprepared when his lips touched hers, his merry eyes smiling down into hers. She was even more unprepared for the sense of longing that swept through her and the way her arms seemed to wrap themselves around his neck of their own accord.

All thoughts of Lady Pinkwell were swept away. All fears about the future as well. Even the knowledge that Mr. Talbot had come to take her to a salon and that his mother must be waiting outside in the carriage was banished from Penelope's mind.

Here, now, this moment as he drew her close against him and feathered kisses on her face was all she could think of. All she wished to think of.

Penelope clung to Mr. Talbot with a need, a desire, she could not have guessed was part of her. And when he let her go, she stared up at him, dazed, an uncertain smile upon her face to match the brilliant one on his.

And then he dashed everything by saying brightly, "There. Now that ought to convince you I like women."

Instantly Penelope was out of his arms and backing away from him. Her anger at Lady Pinkwell was nothing to the rage she felt toward Mr. Talbot.

"Was that what you intended?" she demanded. "To persuade me I have mistaken your character? What a pity, then, that you were so inept!"

And then, before she could disgrace herself by crying in front of him, Penelope turned and fled the room.

He had made a disaster of things. An utter disaster of things, Geoffrey thought with despair. All it wanted was a witness to make the disaster complete.

Somehow he was not surprised to look up and discover Miss Tibbles standing in the doorway watching him. Nor to have her advance and close the door behind her.

"I will not ask why you believe Lady Penelope needs to be persuaded you like women. What I will say is that was not well done of you," she observed tartly.

"Thank you, I had already perceived that myself," he retorted, just as tartly.

"Mind you"—she continued to advance—"I am not certain whether I should scold you more for your clumsiness in speaking to Lady Penelope as you did, or for the kisses which preceded it. I am not sure which was the greater folly. Or the greater impropriety."

Geoffrey Talbot knew when he was beaten. He dropped his head into his hands and said, "Go ahead, ring a peal over my head. You cannot say anything worse to me than I am already thinking."

"I doubt that very much," Miss Tibbles said dryly. "However, I have no wish to waste my breath, as I undoubtedly shall if I, as you say, ring a peal over your head."

He looked at her then and said, an imp of mischief starting to raise its head, "Why are you here, then? To throw me out?"

"That I should leave to the footmen, if it came to the point. No, I am here to help you, if you have the wit to listen."

Geoffrey stared at the governess suspiciously. "Why?" he demanded.

"I have told you before, Lady Penelope's happiness is very important to me," Miss Tibbles retorted. "And the only chance for that, so far as I can see, is if someone gives you lessons in common sense when it comes to dealing with women."

What did he have to lose? Geoffrey grinned and invited Miss Tibbles to sit with a gesture of his hand. When they were both settled he said, "Very well, I am yours to instruct."

He thought he heard her snort a very unladylike snort but he pretended not to notice.

"You came to take Lady Penelope to a literary salon. Do so. And cease trying to persuade her of anything. Simply be a considerate companion to her and allow her to begin to pursue you."

"Excellent advice save that I doubt very much she will go," Geoffrey said gloomily.

Miss Tibbles smiled a wintry smile. "Leave that to me," she said.

Penelope did not wish to go to a salon with Mr. Talbot. Not when her feelings were in such a muddled state as they were just now. She had been certain, for so long, that she never wished to marry, but Mr. Talbot's kisses were changing everything.

They were meant to deceive her, and instead they were touching her heart and her soul in a way she had not known possible. She found herself wanting to kiss Mr. Talbot again. Not that she would, she told herself. And yet, just the wanting appalled her.

Still, when Miss Tibbles came to tell her that Mr. Talbot had not left but was waiting to take her to the salon, Penelope dared not refuse. Not when the governess had such a stern look in her eyes. Better to escape from the scolding she would otherwise receive, even if it did mean finding herself in Mr. Talbot's company once again.

At least Lady Talbot was waiting in the carriage and Penelope could focus her attention on her. They talked of the book of poetry Lady Talbot had lent her.

Mr. Talbot peered at the book. "Was that written by a woman?" he asked with some surprise. When she nodded he said, "How unusual."

Lady Talbot glared at her son. "How can you say so after all the salons we have been to? There are many lady poets. By now you must know that not everyone lives within the strictures society sets for women."

Penelope felt a flush creep up her cheeks. Could Lady Talbot have guessed what a rebel she was? Well, of course she had, for Penelope made no secret of it. But had she, could she, guess how far beyond the line her wayward emotions wished to take her? And with Mr. Talbot?

But if she could, Lady Talbot betrayed no hint of censure in her manner. Instead she talked lightly of poets like Jane Taylor and Felicia Hemans and Mathilda Betham. She talked until Mr. Talbot became impatient.

He had been thumbing through the book, reading here and there, and now he said, "Yes, yes, but surely one could do better than this? Why this poet writes of such trivial matters!"

For the first time, Penelope saw Lady Talbot angry, truly angry. "Indeed? Trivial because they write of the subject of women's lives? Trivial because they write differently from men? Do not, I beg of you, speak such nonsense here today," Lady Talbot said in a chilling voice, "otherwise you will expose your foolishness to everyone present and I pray you will spare me that embarrassment."

Penelope watched, waiting for Mr. Talbot to dismiss his mother's words impatiently. She waited for him to grow angry, as her father would have done. She waited for him to make some condescending remark.

He did none of these things. Instead he stared, long and hard, at his mother. His brows drew together in a frown. He opened his mouth to speak several times and then closed it again. Finally he smiled that oddly endearing smile of his and said, "Will it satisfy you if I promise to try to listen today with an open mind?"

Lady Talbot's anger faded as quickly as it had come. Her own smile matched her son's and she reached out a hand to touch his cheek.

"It is all I have ever asked of you. Or your father. You, at least have listened."

Penelope felt her anger melt away. How could she be angry with someone who answered as Mr. Talbot had? A look passed between Lady Talbot and her son, one that Penelope would have given a great deal to be able to understand. But before she could ask any questions, even if she had dared, the carriage stopped and it was time to alight. Perhaps, she thought, there would be a chance to ask about his father later.

But there was not. And in truth, by the time they left the salon, Penelope's thoughts were so taken up by what she had heard and seen that she forgot to wonder.

*   *   *

Geoffrey expected Lady Penelope to desert him the moment they entered the salon. But she did not. To his surprise, she stayed by his side instead of moving away to seek other company. He began to hope that he had not damaged his position irretrievably after all.

Unfortunately, other people noticed. It would not have been so bad had Lady Pinkwell not overset Lady Penelope earlier. As it was, however, Geoffrey could have strangled the person who said, in her hearing, "Good lord! It seems the Ice Princess is melting. Did anyone ever think to see such a thing?"

The titters that followed did not help matters.

They were laughing at her. It was not the first time it had happened, but today it was more than Penelope could bear. Particularly to have it happen here, where she had once thought everyone would be above such things. She wanted to turn and flee.

But then Mr. Talbot placed a hand over hers and smiled down at her with such a warm, understanding smile that all her anger melted away. Almost she swayed toward him, and would surely have done so had they not been in such a public place.

"They are ninnies," he whispered, "pay them no mind."

Penelope looked up at Mr. Talbot and said, "It must be difficult for you, as well."

"On the contrary," he said with that smile she could not resist, "everyone envies me."

But Penelope knew only too well that many did not envy Mr. Talbot, that they thought him a fool.

He touched the side of her face. "Please," he said softly, with infinite gentleness, "do not let them disconcert you. I am very well pleased with our betrothal."

And somehow that made everything seem all right. For the moment, anyway.

It was only when she was home, in the safety and privacy of her room, that Penelope worried again. Was she a fool for feeling this way about a man who could not love her? And what about his kisses? And her response to them? Or her secret hope that he would kiss her again?

Was there something wrong with her that she should wish for such a breach of propriety? Or did other young ladies feel this way as well? Who could she ask?

Her sister Barbara! The thought came to Penelope in a flash. *She* had gone beyond the line of propriety, far beyond, before her betrothal to Lord Farrington. Surely she would understand. Perhaps she could tell Penelope how better to guard her heart, how better to rule her emotions.

The more she thought about it, the more it seemed to Penelope that Barbara would be the perfect one to advise her in her present situation.

She did, briefly, consider asking Miss Tibbles. But even after four years, she still found that redoubtable woman daunting. And she had a shrewd notion she might not like what Miss Tibbles had to say.

No, better to seek out Barbara and ask her what she thought. And how could Mama or Aunt Ariana object? It was, after all, perfectly unexceptionable for a young lady to visit her sister, wasn't it?

Penelope sat down at her writing desk and wrote a brief note to her sister, asking when it would be convenient for her to come around. The note was quickly dispatched and a reply received quickly. Lady Farrington would be delighted to see her sister tomorrow morning, if she would care to come then.

She would rather not have had to wait, but then it was a small matter. And it would give her time to collect her thoughts so that when she did see Barbara, she would know precisely what she wished to ask her. Meanwhile, she could dream of the kisses Mr. Talbot had given her. And imagine that she was kissing him back. Again.

Chapter 13

Lady Farrington was most intrigued to hear from her sister, Penelope. She greeted her the next morning with outstretched hands, having taken care to dispatch Lord Farrington out of the way. For, as she told him frankly, "We shall be talking about matters of the heart, my dear, and I cannot help thinking that Penelope will speak more openly if you are not there. You would only contrive to put her out of countenance, you know."

His eyes twinkling, he gravely agreed to go. "So long as you give me your full attention later, my love," he added compellingly.

Lady Farrington blushed. She might be in the latter stages of impending childbirth, but he still could warm her with a look. And although she could not understand how it was possible, he still seemed to find her as attractive as ever. Something he contrived to prove to her, every chance he got. Chances that Lady Farrington was very careful to make certain happened frequently.

But now her thoughts were on Penelope. She noted the wistful look in her sister's eyes, the becoming blush in her cheeks, even the careful way she had arranged her hair when, in the past, she had always said she had no patience for such nonsense. Clearly something very interesting was happening here.

"It would appear, my dear sister, that being betrothed is very agreeable to you," Lady Farrington observed dryly.

The blush deepened. "Well, you see, Barbara, that is precisely why I am here," Penelope confided naively. "I am utterly confused and don't know what to do."

This last was said with a wail and Lady Farrington permitted herself a tiny smile. "Yes, I imagine you are," she said equably. "I thought you must be, the moment I heard of your betrothal. I would have come to see you at once but I am supposed to stay at home, as much as possible, for the next few weeks. So tell me all about this Mr. Talbot, to whom you have become betrothed."

Penelope did so, omitting certain details. She concluded by saying, "I am very confused, Barbara. I was certain I did not wish to be married, but now I wonder. And I wonder about myself. That I find myself imagining Mr. Talbot embracing me. Barbara, is there something terribly wrong with me?"

Lady Farrington suppressed the laughter that threatened to bubble up inside of her. It was amusing and yet, at the same time, she understood only too well the confusion her sister felt. The question was, how best to answer her.

Barbara chose her words carefully. "It is not in the least unnatural to imagine such things when one is, well, drawn to a gentleman. As I presume you must be drawn to Mr. Talbot, or you would not have agreed to marry him. As for your uncertainty, that, too, is natural. Even on my wedding day I had moments when I thought I must cry off."

Penelope was silent. She did not at once answer her sister and Barbara knew, then, that there was a great deal Penelope was not telling her.

"Come, dear, what is it?" she asked soothingly. "Did Mama and Papa force you to this match?"

Now Penelope met her sister's eyes squarely. "In a manner of speaking," she said slowly. "I agreed to this betrothal because I was so tired of being told I must marry someone. But I thought, then, that I need not actually go through with it, in the end."

Barbara drew in her breath sharply, understanding completely what such a thing would mean. "And now you think you must?" she prompted her sister.

Penelope hesitated then said, "Not that I must, but perhaps that I wish to do so."

"Then what is the problem?" Barbara asked, bewildered.

"Two things," Penelope replied. "One is that I am still afraid of losing myself, should I marry. And the other is that I am not in the least certain Mr. Talbot will agree to do so!"

Barbara gaped at her sister. "I am feeling very stupid," she said slowly, "but I do not understand. If Mr. Talbot asked you to marry him, he cannot simply cry off. And surely, if he asked you, he must wish to marry you. Unless you have had a falling out with him?"

Penelope shook her head. She decided, apparently, that honesty was called for and she told Barbara the bargain they had made between them.

"Yes, I see. It is the devil of a coil," her sister agreed.

Penelope rose and walked over to the window. She looked down on the busy street below as she said, over her shoulder, carelessly, "It is even worse, Barbara, since I think Mr. Talbot may be very much like Uncle Frederick."

Again Lady Farrington drew in her breath in dismay. "Dear heavens, Penelope!" she exclaimed.

Now Penelope turned to face her sister. "Don't you dare say a word against Uncle Frederick," she said fiercely. "I know that no one else in the family will speak of him, nor will they forgive him for refusing to marry. But I have no patience for such nonsense. I like Uncle Frederick. And I like Mr. Talbot. Very much."

"You have lost your heart to him," Barbara said, and it was not a question. "Well, you had best come and sit down and let us talk about it. Is there any chance he might come to like you?"

Penelope reluctantly took the seat her sister indicated. She clasped her hands in her lap as she said, "There are times when I think he might. And yesterday he even kissed me."

The look on Lady Farrington's face was comical. She did not know whether to remonstrate on the impropriety or cheer this possible signal that Mr. Talbot's dislike of women was not so complete after all. Penelope's next words dashed that hope, however.

"He did it to prove me mistaken in my belief he was like Uncle Frederick," she said bitterly. "He told me so himself. But I, fool that I am, found it much too wonderful."

Barbara put a hand over Penelope's. "Dearest, you must take one day at a time, while you decide what to do. Perhaps Mr. Talbot will discover that he does like you, if you give him sufficient reason to. Be as agreeable as you can and see what happens."

Penelope shook her head. "I cannot be other than myself," she said sadly. Then, drawing in a deep breath, she rose to her feet. "I must be going. But first, tell me how you are doing."

Lady Farrington made a wry face. "Feeling very clumsy and awkward right now. And this child does not know how to rest. He kicks me constantly. But I am more happy, I think, than I have ever been."

The look of pleasure on Barbara's face stayed with Penelope long after she left. In a way it reassured her for, a few years before, Penelope could not have imagined her sister so content for any reason, much less for being a wife and, soon, a mother.

As for Barbara, she watched Penelope go and felt for her. It was not an easy situation in which she found herself. Suddenly she wished very much to see Damian.

As if he had read her mind, Lord Farrington came into the room then. He sat beside her and kissed her fingertips and said, "So, tell me, how is your sister?"

But Lady Farrington now had other things on her mind and it was some time before she thought to answer his question.

On the other side of town, early that afternoon, Lord Talbot climbed down from his traveling coach and brushed the dirt from his coat. He then marched up to the front door of his town house and rapped smartly on the door. It was opened at once and a startled footman gazed bemused as his lordship brushed past, tossing his hat, gloves, and cane onto the table in the foyer.

"Is her ladyship in? Of course she must be," he said without waiting for an answer. "No, no, you needn't bother to announce me. I shall go straight up."

"But sir, who are you?" the befuddled footman asked helplessly.

Instantly he was hushed by the majordomo, who said swiftly, "Forgive him, m'lord, he is new. This," he told the hapless footman, "is Lord Talbot, master of this household. Her ladyship will be delighted to see you, m'lord. You will find her in the sunroom."

"Doubt she'll be delighted, but nothing she can do about the matter," Talbot countered. "I'm here and not like to leave soon."

Both servants pretended not to have heard this unbecoming frankness. Instead the footman made haste to collect the hat, gloves, and cane as his superior led the way upstairs, despite Lord Talbot's assurances that there was no need for him to do so.

"But my lord, surely you and her ladyship will wish refreshments," the majordomo said, determined not to miss what promised to be a fascinating reunion between his master and mistress.

The diversion was successful. "By Jove, you've the right of it! Famished. I am absolutely famished," his lordship exclaimed.

And that, his majordomo thought dryly, was definitely preferable to his lordship announcing he was wishful for something to drink.

Upstairs, the reunion was all that the man could have hoped for. Lord Talbot hurried ahead of his servant and threw open the door to the sunroom himself.

"Lydia! I'm here!" he announced gleefully.

Lady Talbot promptly dropped the teacup she was holding. It shattered on the floor, unnoticed at her feet. "Edward," she said, her voice quavering only sightly. "What a surprise."

"Didn't expect to see me here, did you?" Lord Talbot asked jovially, bounding over to plant a salute on his wife's bemused brow.

"No, I did not," she agreed faintly.

"You ought to have," he said, wagging a finger at her. "M'son gets betrothed, I ought to be here."

There was nothing that could be said to that and Lady Talbot did not even try. Instead she looked over at the majordomo standing in the doorway of the room.

Instantly he came to her rescue. "Did you wish refreshments, m'lord? M'lady?" he inquired. "Shall I have dinner put forward? What do you wish me to say to any callers?"

As she settled these domestic questions, Lady Talbot regained a little of her composure. And by the time she was done, she was able to turn to her husband and smile, if rather weakly, at him.

"Well, you are right to want to be here to see Geoffrey wed," she admitted reluctantly. "The difficulty is that the young lady is reluctant to come to the point and set a wedding date."

"Oh, pooh! Nonsense! All young ladies are eager to be married. Geoffrey must be bungling the matter, as usual. Never fear, I shall drop a word in his ear as to how to handle the chit and all will be settled in a trice. That is to say," he said, pausing and frowning, "I presume we *do* wish it settled? The girl is not an antidote? Daughter of an earl, I recall. Not a pauper, is she? Not covered with the pox?"

"Oh, no, not at all. Lady Penelope, Westcott's daughter, is a very lovely young thing," Lady Talbot was happy to be able to reassure him.

"Good. That's all settled then, right and tight. And about time it is, too, that Geoffrey settled down and set up his nursery. Mean to talk to him about that. He won't want me rattling about the old house, once he takes his bride there. No doubt he'll be happy to make me an allowance to live in London and leave the place to him and his bride."

"I am not certain," Lady Talbot said with alarm. "Perhaps he means to live in London with her."

That gave his lordship pause. Clearly he did not like to be balked. But he was an expert at self-deception and, after a moment, waved his hands. "No, no. London is no place for newlyweds. Privacy, that's what they want. No, no, the country house would be much the best thing. Depend upon it, Geoffrey will see the reason in that."

Lady Talbot did not depend on any such thing. Indeed, it was her devout hope that Geoffrey would decree precisely the opposite. The thought of the swath her husband would cut through London, given half a chance, sent chills down her spine and she could not help hoping that Geoffrey would be home soon. And that someone would have the foresight to warn him before he came upstairs.

Even as the thought formed, the door to the sunroom opened again and her son stood in the doorway. His expression was grim as he stared at Lord Talbot.

"Father."

"Geoffrey, my boy! How delightful to see you. And with such news in your pocket! But you ought to have written to tell me yourself," Lord Talbot said, wagging a finger playfully at his son.

"What are you doing here?"

The voice was implacable, harsh in its tones. Lord Talbot did not even seem to notice. He held his arms wide. "But where else would I be, my boy?" he protested. "My son is betrothed. I ought to be at his side, lending him my support. Come, tell me when the wedding is. And if your mother is right and the girl refuses to set a date, we'll put our heads together and contrive something, I promise you."

But that was too much for Geoffrey. He turned on his heel and walked out of the room, letting the door slam shut behind him. He did not see the expression of dismay that crossed his father's face. Nor the way Lord Talbot manfully struggled to change it to a smile for the benefit of his wife.

As for Lady Talbot, she was as close to tears as she had been in some time. And at the moment, she thought, they would have come as a distinct relief.

Even the advent of a cart, with some food for Lord Talbot, could not change the charged atmosphere in the room. Still, Lady Talbot tried.

"He is young. Impatient, Edward. Give him time to come around."

For once her husband looked her directly in the eye and said bluntly, "And you, Lydia? What will it take for you to come around? You cannot claim youth, on your part. And heaven knows you've had sufficient time. Have you come around?"

For a long moment Lady Talbot looked at him and a tear rolled down her cheek. Then slowly she rose to her feet, crossed over to where Lord Talbot sat, and kissed him on the forehead. Then, without a word, she left the room.

Lord Talbot gazed after her and if a tear rolled down his own cheek, there was no one to see.

Chapter 14

Penelope waited all the rest of that day for Mr. Talbot to come to see her. She had not the slightest notion what to make of his behavior the day before. Mr. Talbot had been kind. He had been more than kind.

She could not blame him for trying to deceive her with kisses. In his place she might have done the same. And he was still her friend. She still knew no one else who could enter into her sentiments so entirely. Or speak with her so freely on matters everyone else considered most unsuitable for women. No one else who understood her thirst for learning.

So now Penelope wore her prettiest dress, pinched her cheeks, and prepared just what she would say on a number of suitably intellectual topics. She would not, of course, allow Mr. Talbot to take liberties again. Indeed, she would make it plain to him that such pretense, on his part, was entirely unnecessary. She would make it plain to him they were still friends.

But she had no chance. He did not come. Early afternoon became late afternoon. Mama tried to reassure her.

"No doubt he had some business affairs to attend to," she said with a little laugh.

"You must not expect him to sit in your pocket, you know," her aunt added tartly. "Men abominate women who do so. When he does come, you must greet him with every appearance of complacence."

The hours passed and still he did not come.

"He was supposed to come at two," Penelope said softly, when it was almost three and they were between callers.

"Perhaps he forgot?" Lady Westcott suggested.

Aunt Ariana was more blunt. "If you have driven him away with some of your nonsense, you will come to regret it, Penelope. Gentlemen of his kind nature, who have pockets as deep as his, are rarely come by, even for the daughter of an earl."

Only Lord Westcott was not alarmed, when he wandered into the drawing room, sometime later.

"Oh, pooh!" he said. "Man misses one day calling on his betrothed and you, all of you, start to run about clucking disaster. Why, Delwinia, when I was courting you, I daresay I didn't come by above two or three times a week!"

Lady Westcott smiled but there was no use trying to explain to him how different it was with Mr. Talbot, how intently he had courted Penelope, choosing to spend time by her side every day since the betrothal. Perhaps it was mere foolishness on their part to worry, but after so much trouble to bring Penelope to this point, the thought that it might yet all fall apart was more than she could bear.

As for Penelope, she discovered as she waited that somehow, in some way, when she was not watching, Mr. Talbot had become unaccountably necessary to her comfort and her happiness. It was a thought which ought to have frightened her. It was a thought that, beforehand, she would have sworn would bring her to choose a fight with the man the moment he appeared. It was a thought which made her hope instead that he would walk in the door at any moment, with a smile in his eyes and a cocky grin on his face, and a ready explanation for everything.

And still he did not come.

Across town, Geoffrey Talbot woke with a throbbing headache. His first thought was to wonder what the devil had happened to him. His second was to bound out of bed, ring vigorously for his valet, and demand, the instant the fellow appeared, to know if his father was still in the house.

Dantry had been with Talbot a long time. He exchanged a significant look with Geoffrey and said carefully, "Indeed, I believe his lordship to be sleeping even later than yourself. Had it been otherwise, I should have awakened you at once, I assure you."

"Good man!"

Dantry hesitated, then added, "If you hurry, my lord, you may see your mother as she sits down to a neat luncheon that has been set out in the dining room."

Geoffrey groaned. "As late as that, is it?" he asked.

Dantry nodded. "Later," he said. "Her ladyship had the luncheon set back twice."

With a speed that would have appalled most valets, Geoffrey washed and dressed. Dantry knew too well the reasons for such haste to object. And indeed, when one had a master as well turned out as Mr. Talbot, it was easy to allow him haste. He had no need to take precious time to correct faults. Even the careless way he dropped his chin to set his neckcloth worked perfectly. Not for him the need to spend an hour or more tying it just so.

With justifiable pride, Dantry watched Mr. Talbot leave his dressing room exquisitely attired. It was most definitely a pleasure to look after such a fine gentleman. Mr. Talbot might be more inclined to intellectual pursuits than creating a social dash, but that did not mean he tolerated disarray in his person. A circumstance for which Dantry was profoundly grateful.

Downstairs, Geoffrey reached the dining room at almost the same moment as his mother. In her eyes he could see a weariness and a sadness that mirrored his own.

"Was it very bad?" she asked.

Geoffrey shrugged, determined not to worry her. "Not until the early hours of the morning, when he began to lose.

He objected greatly when I refused to frank his vowels, and so did some of the gentlemen he was gaming with."

She nodded. Then, her face very white, she asked, "And women?"

Now Geoffrey dropped the plate he was filling onto the sideboard and went around to hug his mother. "You know I would never let him do so when I was there."

She tried to smile. "I did not know if you could stop him."

"When his pockets are to let, very easily," Geoffrey said grimly.

Even as he finished speaking, the object of his disapproval appeared in the doorway of the dining room. He did not look as neatly turned out as Geoffrey, but then Lord Talbot's intent had clearly been to reach the dining room at all costs while his wife and son were still there.

The moment he saw them, he began his recriminations. "A fine thing," he said, with an air of injury, "when m'wife sets my son to spy on me. And he, unfeeling creature, refuses to vouch for my trifling debts!"

"They were not trifling," Geoffrey snapped back, "or would not have been had I let you gamble on."

Lord Talbot advanced into the room. Clearly he was in a fighting mood. "I would not have to look to you to vouch for them if matters had been settled in an ordinary way. Your uncle ought to have left me his funds, not you. It was dashed improper for him to do otherwise. And as for your grandmother, we shall not speak of her at all!"

"Perhaps your mother knew you too well," Geoffrey answered evenly.

Lady Talbot held out a hand to remonstrate. Both men ignored her.

"You have never given me the respect I deserve," Lord Talbot said in an aggrieved tone.

"On the contrary," Geoffrey shot back, "you have never earned it."

"Ungrateful whelp! I ought to have raised you better."

"That is the one point on which we can both agree. Your failure as a father!"

For a brief moment they glared at one another, then Lord Talbot sank into a chair and dropped his head into his hands. "You hate me, the pair of you. And I can scarcely say I blame you."

Lady Talbot started to speak but Geoffrey forestalled her. There was no pity, no kindness in his voice as he said sardonically, "If we do, Father, it is because you have given us no other choice."

And then he stalked from the room.

Behind him, he could already hear his mother making soothing sounds. And because it was more than he could bear, he fled the house.

Geoffrey would have gone to Lady Penelope. It was his first thought. He wanted to pour his heart out to her. But common sense prevailed. He could not tell her what he and his mother had been at such pains to conceal all these years.

Nor could he bear, he realized, to see the wariness come into her own eyes as she compared Lord Talbot to himself. Would she worry that he would be the same? If so, Geoffrey could not blame her. There were times he had that fear himself.

He didn't truly think so, or he would never have contemplated marriage at all. But his other relatives were sound, and he took heart in that. If only the one false one had not happened to be his father.

Geoffrey walked, not even seeing where he went. All thoughts of his appointment with Lady Penelope were forgotten. If he had remembered, he would have cried off. He could not face her now.

But his thoughts were filled with the bitter realization that he must be back home by nightfall, when Lord Talbot would no doubt choose to go out again. And he would have to be there to go with him.

Geoffrey wanted to curse. He felt a moment's impulse, but that was all it was, to try to drown his sorrows in drink. He wished, without being able to think of any, that there were some way to reach oblivion that did not include behaving like his father.

Instead he walked for hours and then turned homeward again.

Earlier that day, in another part of town, Frederick Baines climbed down from his coach and looked around, prepared to be pleased. And he was. The bustle about the little hotel, The White Stallion, intrigued him, as it did every time he came to London. It was a small place, but an elegant one, and it catered mostly to gentlemen who preferred the quiet of The White Stallion to the bustle of larger hostelries such as the Clarendon.

The clerks greeted Mr. Baines with suitable deference and informed him that his favorite room was ready. His valet, Matthew, undertook to supervise the removal of the luggage from his coach to the hotel and Frederick had nothing to do but please himself. Which he did.

He made arrangements for his dinner, then changed out of his traveling clothes and set out to enjoy the afternoon. He had no doubt that if he looked, he would find any number of friends in their usual haunts and by evening would have all the information that could be gleaned about Mr. Talbot, his niece's putative fiancé.

Whether Mr. Talbot would continue to be her fiancé remained to be seen, but it was never Mr. Baines's practice to judge someone sight unseen. Nor to act without giving the person the benefit of the doubt. Neither, however, did he believe everything that was said to him and he did like to have his information collected beforehand.

This thoroughness was one of the reasons Mr. Baines had been so useful in the Mediterranean, some fifteen or more years earlier. Few knew of his involvement there, but those who did had very real reason to be grateful to him.

So Baines applied the same methods now. In the course of the afternoon, he talked to a great many people. He even managed to track down Mr. Manton and they had a most interesting conversation together. One that left Frederick Baines more bemused than ever. Clearly he was going to have to see Mr. Talbot for himself.

He knew something of Lord Talbot, knew him to be a shocking loose screw. If the son was the same . . .

But there was no reason to think so, Baines told himself. Indeed most reports of the boy had been remarkably favorable. Still, apparently Lord Talbot was in London and both father and son had gone rakehelling the night before. That news did *not* please Uncle Frederick.

Geoffrey composed the note in haste. Any moment now his father would insist on going out the door. But he had to write and tell Lady Penelope something. He knew only too well how cruel the tattle-mongers could be, and their tongues would be wagging when he did not show his face at Almack's tonight. When he was not there to dance with her.

And yet what could he say? He settled for something less than what was in his heart, but something more, perhaps, than she expected.

Lady Penelope,
    I cannot be at Almack's tonight, but believe that I wish I could be and shall be thinking of you.
                    Yours,
                        The Honorable Geoffrey Talbot

With the note, Geoffrey included a book he had found, just two days ago, and thought she would like. He had meant to give it to Lady Penelope in person but since he could not say when he would next be able to see her, this would have to do.

For a moment, Talbot allowed himself to feel abused. All the rage he was accustomed to feeling toward his father came back in full force.

But it could not last long. His father was as he was and it was his responsibility to keep a rein on him. There was no use repining over what he could not change.

Geoffrey looked once more at the book and smiled. He could not help but believe that a book would be more acceptable to Lady Penelope than any other present he could have sent. And this one should please her more than most, as it was a scientific discourse.

He only hoped it would be enough to let her forgive him for not being with her tonight.

But there was his father, ready to set out on his rounds again tonight. And he had to go with him. A footman would deliver the note and book and he would go and try to keep his father safe. For one more night.

Chapter 15

Geoffrey Talbot was not in a very good mood. To be sure, he had managed to get his father home early, by dint of both threats and blatant bribery. But even so, by then it was too late to go to Almack's, which is where he knew his betrothed to be.

He wondered if she had gotten his note. He wondered what she had thought of the book. He wondered if she had forgiven him for failing to call on her at two in the afternoon. For by now, and much too late, he remembered that he had promised to do so.

Geoffrey was neither in high spirits nor a pleasant mood. He walked into White's practically spoiling for a fight even though he knew he could not, would not, allow himself to indulge in one.

"Mr. Talbot?"

He paused and looked at the slightly plump gentleman standing before him. The fellow was looking him up and down through a quizzing glass with a faint air of both bemusement and appraisal in his gaze.

"Yes?"

The gentleman tsked. He shook his head. "No, no, m'boy, you ought to be more respectful to your elders. But never mind. You don't know who the devil I may be. And I have the advantage of you for I know a great deal about you. Might we perhaps find somewhere to talk and rectify this disparity? I promise you, it is in your interest to do so."

Geoffrey sighed. He was really very tired. Still, he found he could not refuse the gentleman who was gazing up at him so earnestly and with such a merry twinkle in his eye. So he gestured toward another room and said, "I think we may be private in there."

The gentleman followed Geoffrey's lead, content to remain silent until they could both be certain they would not be overheard. Talbot waited courteously until the older man was seated, then he sat opposite him. Despite himself, he began to be intrigued.

"May I ask who you are?" he said.

"Frederick Baines."

For a moment, the name meant nothing to Geoffrey. Then, with a sinking sensation, he said, "Uncle Frederick?"

The gentleman let the smile broaden. "Some might call me so. Particularly my niece, Lady Penelope, with whom I believe you are a little acquainted?"

"I am betrothed to her, as you very well know!" Geoffrey said gruffly. "I hope you don't think I mean to ask your approval for I already have that from her father."

Baines tapped the tips of his fingers together, steepled in front of his face. "Mmm," he said cautiously. "Nevertheless I do have some, shall we say, influence with my niece."

Geoffrey frowned. The man before him did not seem to be radiating disapproval. On the other hand, neither did he appear to approve.

"What do you wish of me?" he asked.

Uncle Frederick waved a hand. "Oh, a few questions answered. Nothing very difficult, I assure you."

Geoffrey quirked an eyebrow in disbelief. Still, he was prepared to play the game.

"What do you wish to know?" he asked blandly.

Uncle Frederick told him.

* * *

"Penelope, if you do not this instant sit down, I shall strangle you!" Lady Westcott said impatiently. "Either Mr. Talbot will come today or he will not."

"And if he does not, someone else will, depend upon it," Lady Brisbane said grimly. "If one lady asked me where Mr. Talbot was, last night at Almack's, I daresay fifty did so. He really ought to have been there."

Penelope looked down at the book in her hands and resisted the impulse to hug it close to her. She was oddly touched that Mr. Talbot had sent it to her. He was the only man, indeed the only person of her acquaintance who would have understood that she would love a present like this far more than any conventional gift.

It was so like him to understand, that Penelope found herself smiling oddly at it. Still, she must be careful. If either her mother or aunt noticed, it would only invite questions. Questions she did not know how to answer, nor did she wish to try.

Why had Mr. Talbot sent this book, however dear it might be to her, instead of bringing it around himself? Why were there so many whispers, last night, that he had been seen, the night before, in the worst gaming hells of the city? And where was he today?

As her aunt and mother continued to speculate, Penelope clenched her hands together in her lap to keep from jumping up again and this time it was her mother who did so.

Lady Westcott peered out the window as if this might cause Mr. Talbot to appear. Instead, she gave a tiny gasp and said in a rather strangled voice, "Ariana, I do believe Frederick has come to call."

"Oh, no! Just what we need to really set tongues wagging even more," Lady Brisbane moaned. "Perhaps you are mistaken and it merely looks like Frederick, from up here?"

"No, it is certainly he," Lady Westcott said mournfully.

But this was too much for Penelope. With a martial glint in her eye, she said with loud determination, "I like Uncle Frederick."

"Of course you do," Lady Brisbane agreed. "Frederick is a very likable man. But what has that to say to the point? He will still draw the gossips down upon our heads."

"Yes, asking when Frederick plans to marry, and always said with such a knowing look in their eyes," Lady Westcott added in the same mournful voice as before. "And I never know which way to look. It is not as if Frederick even tries to pretend."

"Well, why should he?" Penelope demanded hotly.

But her aunt and mother merely looked at one another and shook their heads. Which perhaps was just as well, for as they did so, Jeffries threw open the door of the drawing room and announced, "The Honorable Frederick Baines."

Penelope at once rose to greet him, a broad smile upon her face. "Uncle Frederick! I am so happy to see you."

"And I to see you, puss," he said, kissing her cheek. "Halloo, Ariana. Delwinia. You both look to be in excellent spirits."

"We are," Lady Westcott said uncertainly.

"Of course we are," Ariana chimed in, more firmly. "But whatever are you doing here?"

Frederick smiled sleepily at his sisters and took a chair opposite them. He waved his hand one way, then the other. "Oh, this and that. And of course, since I have come to London, I had to see my niece and congratulate her on her betrothal."

"Do you approve then, Uncle Frederick?" Penelope asked anxiously.

"It is not for Frederick to approve or disapprove!" Lady Westcott said in shocked tones. "That is for your father to say."

"I must say, it is nonsensical, above half, for you to come

and stick your oar into things now, Frederick," Lady Brisbane said with a sniff.

Frederick allowed himself to take a pinch of snuff before he answered. And when he did so, he grinned. "Oh, I don't claim to have any authority in the matter. Or even any great interest. But I did happen to meet Mr. Talbot and thought I would come around and tell Penelope so."

"And?" she asked eagerly.

Silence. All three ladies looked expectantly at Frederick. He chuckled. Finally he decided to put them out of their misery and answer. "I think you are in for some surprises, Penelope," he said.

"Oh, no!" Lady Westcott moaned.

For the first time, Frederick lost his look of good humor. "Don't be a ninny!" he told his sister sharply. "I didn't mean that. In fact, quite the contrary."

As both Lady Westcott and Lady Brisbane drew a deep breath of relief, Frederick turned to Penelope and said slowly, to make certain she understood, "I think, puss, you will find he likes women far better than you realize. And I don't"—he spoke pointedly, to forestall Lady Brisbane—"mean that he likes them too well."

Then, because Penelope still looked puzzled, he added significantly, "Mr. Talbot, my dear, has nothing in common with myself or Mr. Manton."

Now she understood. She went very pale. Then her cheeks flushed with color. Finally, her eyes sparkled with anger and she rose to her feet.

"How dare he?" she demanded, beginning to pace back and forth.

"How dare he what?" Lady Westcott asked, bewildered. "What are the pair of you talking about?"

Quicker than her sister, Lady Brisbane planted herself in front of Penelope and demanded, "Do I understand that you thought he was like Frederick?"

But Penelope was far too shrewd to admit to any such thing. Or to stay around and answer. Leaving the book Mr. Talbot had sent her on the chair where she had set it when she stood up, she headed for the doorway.

"I think," Penelope said quickly, "there is something I need to do—above stairs. It was wonderful to see you, Uncle Frederick. Perhaps you would come round and take me for a drive later this afternoon?"

He chuckled again as he rose to his feet. "Oh, I rather think young Talbot will be around to do that," he said. "But we shall definitely talk further. Come, walk your old uncle out to his carriage."

She took his arm, quickly enough, before her mother or aunt could recover sufficiently to forbid it. Both she and her uncle were conscious of how little time they had and neither wasted any of it.

"Did he tell you he was like me?" Frederick asked shrewdly as they left the drawing room.

"No. But it seemed so obvious."

It was his turn to snort in disbelief. "After the experience of your sisters," he said, "I should think you would know better than to trust the obvious."

"I shall never forgive him for this," Penelope muttered, ignoring the chide.

Uncle Frederick looked surprised. "You may wish to re-consider that," he told her gently. "I should say, short as my acquaintance with him has been, that Mr. Talbot is a good man."

"Yes. Man." Penelope all but spat the word. "That is precisely what I object to. And if I had had any doubts about the matter, he has proved my very point by deceiving me like this!"

Frederick knew the ladies of his family too well to quarrel with one in the throes of self-righteous anger. Discretion, he thought, would be the wiser part of valor, for the moment, at any rate. Later he could try to talk with her again. After she saw Mr. Talbot.

Frederick could not help but inwardly chuckle at the thought of how that encounter was likely to go. And he wondered if there were any way to arrange a view of it. Ah, well, she was likely to tell him every detail the next time he saw her anyway. And with that he decided to be content. If Mr. Talbot could not handle matters himself, he was not half the man Baines took him to be.

Unfortunately, he did not fully take into account Lord Talbot's activities and how long they would require Mr. Talbot's attention. But even if he had, Uncle Frederick would still not have interfered. At least, not yet.

Alone in the house, Penelope slowly, and as quietly as she could, climbed the stairs up to her room. She wanted to hold onto her anger with Mr. Talbot. She wanted to remember that he had deceived her and that on no account should she be willing to receive him again.

Instead, her treacherous heart kept remembering all the times he had been kind to her. All the salons he had taken her to. And how completely he had entered into her sentiments on so many things.

There was even a part of her heart that whispered she could be happy, if only she would allow herself to take the chance. It was the part of her which longed for him to kiss her again. The part of her which had written to ask if ever a man like Uncle Frederick could learn to love a lady. It was the part of her which whispered that since he was not like Uncle Frederick, perhaps Mr. Talbot already had.

Chapter 16

Had he come at once, Geoffrey Talbot might have found Lady Penelope willing to listen to him. He might have found her able to understand and forgive.

But he didn't come at once. She waited and waited and could only grow more angry, particularly as her family, aghast to realize what she had thought, rang peal after peal over her head. This was not something Penelope could be expected to accept with complacence.

By the time he arrived at Lady Brisbane's town house, Geoffrey Talbot was more than two days late and Penelope in no mood to hear anything he wished to say to her. The past two days had been a reminder of all the evils and heartache a man could cause and she wanted no part of him.

Lady Penelope refused to speak to Mr. Talbot when he finally did come. She turned instead to her other guests. He retreated, puzzled, but presuming it was nothing more than pique at his temporary disappearance. In fact, he was so foolish as to consider her anger a good sign.

Since the book seemed not to have pleased her, he brought her flowers. She threw them out the window. He purchased a lovely fan. She snapped it in two and threw the pieces in his face. He tried to coax her with the promise of a drive in the park and finally, she seemed to relent.

"Oh, I shall be delighted to go for a drive in the park with you," Penelope said with a sweetness which ought to have been sufficient to send him running the other way, "particularly if you will set your groom down so that we may speak with perfect privacy."

"Of course," he said, thinking he could all the better coax her into a happier mood.

The moment they reached the park, however, and he set down his groom, Geoffrey Talbot discovered his error. His usually gentle, albeit contrary, Lady Penelope suddenly became a raging virago.

"How dare you lie to me?" she demanded. "Pretending not to like women! Letting me think you were like my Uncle Frederick when he tells me you are not! Letting me think I was safe with you, when all the while you actually like women very well!"

"But I tried to tell you the truth," Geoffrey protested.

"But you knew I didn't believe you."

"What was I to do?" he demanded with pardonable exasperation. "I even kissed you."

"Yes, and then you let me think it was meant to divert me from the truth."

"But I told you it was all a hum. It isn't my fault you didn't believe me," he said with perfect logic.

But Lady Penelope didn't want logic. "How else did you deceive me?" she demanded. "Am I to find out you aren't really opposed to marriage after all?"

And what was he supposed to say to that? Geoffrey turned a bright red and that was quite sufficient to hang him in Penelope's eyes. "You do want to be married!" she gasped. "Oh! I have never been so deceived in my life. Take me straight back home, right this very minute."

"But I thought you were beginning to like me," he protested. "At least a little. And that was why I did it. Because I knew it was the only way you would give me the slightest chance to get to know you. And the only way for you to have the slightest chance to get to know me."

"Take—me—home."

Geoffrey protested. He coaxed. He begged. All to no
avail. Lady Penelope was adamant. Finally, his own temper
beyond controlling, Talbot gritted his teeth, drove around to
where he had left his groom, signaled the man to climb
back up, and then took Lady Penelope home.

They parted on her top step and neither was in a good
mood when they did so.

"You need not call again. I shall tell my parents our betrothal is at an end," she said with a sniff.

"Do so, and you will find yourself hammered at from all
sides," he warned. "Abuse me as much as you like, but
think twice before you cry off. It will only lead to all sorts
of tongues wagging and haranguing from your parents."

"I don't care!"

The door, slammed in his face, led Geoffrey to presume
those were her last words on the matter. Slowly, bitterly, he
went back down the steps. It was all "Uncle Frederick's"
fault, he thought. And with a gleam of anger in his eyes, he
directed his horses in the direction of the small hotel where
Frederick Baines had told Geoffrey he was staying.

Fifteen minutes later, Talbot was pounding on Baines's
door. A rather mincing fellow opened it and said irritably,
"Really, now, we heard you the first time! Must you pound
so loud?"

"Yes, I must," Geoffrey retorted scathingly. "I wish to
see Mr. Baines."

"Well I don't know if he wishes to see you," the fellow
retorted, not taken with Geoffrey's angry face.

"Tell him his niece's ex-fiancé is here and wishes to
speak with him."

The fellow straightened. "Oh, my. Yes, I daresay Mr.
Baines will see you then. Come in. But pray do try not to
raise your voice too loud. We shouldn't want the manage-
ment complaining that we are disturbing the other guests."

Geoffrey quite pithily told the fellow what he thought of

other guests. And then he turned his attention to Frederick Baines, who rose at the sight of him.

"Didn't go well?" Frederick hazarded shrewdly.

"You know damned well it did not! How could it, after you told Lady Penelope the truth about me?"

Another man might have found Geoffrey's fury intimidating. Frederick only grinned. "It is your own fault, you know," he told Talbot, waving him to a chair. "If you hadn't deceived my niece in the first place, you wouldn't be in this fix now."

"If I hadn't deceived her, she would never have agreed to become betrothed to me in the first place!" Geoffrey exploded, still standing.

"Perhaps," Baines conceded. "But I can guess you did not handle it well when she confronted you with the truth."

Talbot flung himself into a chair. "I handled it damnably," he admitted miserably.

Frederick nodded, as though satisfied with something he saw in Talbot's face. "You may still come about," he said. "My niece seems quite taken with you, though I am not certain she has realized that fact herself. But you will get nowhere unless you are honest with her, this time around."

"So I collect."

Frederick hid a smile. "Penelope is not a woman to be ruled," he went on. "You shall have to treat her as someone with a mind equal to your own."

Geoffrey gaped at Baines, though his own mother had said much the same thing to him. "But then how do I make her do as I wish?" he asked.

Now Frederick did grin. "You can't," he said.

You can't. The words still echoed in Geoffrey's ears as he left the hotel. And again as he sat over dinner with his mother and father.

The words even echoed through his thoughts as he followed his father about, later that night, when he should have, might have, under other circumstances, would have been with Lady Penelope. And he didn't like them any better then, than when Frederick Baines had said them the first time.

Penelope did not like having to fight with Mr. Talbot. But how could she overlook such deceit?

"Very easily," her mother said tartly. "All men lie, one time or another."

"You are whistling down the wind a very pretty fortune, an excellent gentleman who desires you, and heaven only knows what else for a silly thing like this?" Lady Brisbane asked with some exasperation.

"It is your own fault for presuming things," Lord Westcott added shortly. "I have no patience with such missishness. You said you would marry him and marry him you shall."

None of which made any impression on Penelope, of course. It was Miss Tibbles who spoke the words that finally captured her attention. And they were spoken in the schoolroom at the top of the house, when no one else was around.

"If your sisters had cried off simply because their husbands had misled them, they would none of them be married now," Miss Tibbles said sensibly. "Do you think any of them regret forgiving the gentleman in question? Do you think any of them would be happier if they had refused to be married? My dear Penelope, men are quite, quite human. They make mistakes, just as we do. Unless you are perfect yourself, what right have you to refuse to forgive him when he clearly wished only happiness for the pair of you?"

Penelope clapped her hands over her ears. She would listen to nothing more. But it was already too late. The words Miss Tibbles had spoken sank deeper and deeper into her consciousness. There was too much truth to them for it to be otherwise.

Besides. There was a corner, and not a tiny one at that, of her heart where she missed him so very much. A part of her that turned, half a dozen times a day to tell Mr. Talbot something, to share a jest which only he would understand. And when she found he was not there, the sense of loss was almost overwhelming.

Nor did it help that her mother and aunt flatly refused to take her to any salons. "Patch up your quarrel with Mr. Talbot," was all they would say when she asked.

By the end of the week no one, seeing Penelope, could doubt the lowering of her spirits. No one had yet sent a notice to the papers saying the betrothal was over, but somehow all of London seemed to know. And people were not kind about it to Penelope.

Gentlemen who had courted her before, pointedly refused to come to her now. Mothers oozed false sympathy over the supposed fact she had been jilted. Other young ladies smiled and merely pretended they didn't know as they asked where Mr. Talbot was tonight.

She gritted her teeth and bore it all, always hoping, though she would not say so even to herself, to catch a glimpse of him. Always hoping that despite her dismissal of him, he would come.

He didn't.

Geoffrey had no notion the trials Penelope was enduring. And even if he had, he could not have been there by her side. He was too busy trying to prevent his father from coming to ruin.

The man refused to listen to reason.

"What the devil do you care? Not only do you have a tidy fortune of your own," Lord Talbot said, when his son tried to bar him from going out, "but you're about to marry a girl who is flush in the pockets as well."

Geoffrey flinched. "No, I'm not."

Lord Talbot goggled at his son. "I know I don't particularly care for gossip and don't listen to it, but I'm sure you are."

"The girl, as you put it, has cried off."

"Well, why did she go and do that?" Lord Talbot demanded. "Not a good thing to do, not good at all." He paused, peered at his son and said shrewdly, "Come over heavy-handed, did you? Foolish boy! Oughtn't to do that until the ceremony is over and all the funds in your hands already."

Geoffrey flushed. He could think of no defense and didn't even try. His father was quick to try to use his perceived advantage.

"Let me talk to the girl. Bound to be able to bring her around. I'll just lie to her. Tell her you're all that is admirable and will make her the perfect husband. Leave it to me. I shall have it all settled again in a trice!" Lord Talbot said eagerly.

"Don't go near her," Geoffrey said through clenched teeth.

Instantly his father retreated. "Oh, as you say. Only wanted to help, my boy. But if you don't want it, I understand completely. Now if you could just see your way clear to lend me a hundred pounds for tonight and let me out the door, we would be even."

Geoffrey shook his head. From the stairway, however, came his mother's voice. "Let him go, Geoffrey," she said quietly. "Sooner or later he will find a way to get out anyway and gamble."

He would have stood firm forever with his father, but he could refuse his mother nothing. Geoffrey moved away from the door.

"The money?" Lord Talbot asked.

Geoffrey merely stared at his father and, after a moment, his lordship shrugged and made good his escape. Talbot closed the door after him. Then he turned to his mother.

"Why did you ask me to let him go?"

There was hurt in his voice and it mirrored the sadness in her eyes. She came down the rest of the way and stopped only inches away from her son.

"Because I have relied on you too long to take care of your father. Because it is time we let him go and do whatever he means to do. We cannot, you cannot, spend your life stopping him. And that is what it would come to."

"By morning he will have lost a fortune," Geoffrey said bitterly.

She nodded. "Perhaps. Or, perhaps he will win. Or come back sooner when he finds his friends reluctant to take his vowels."

"He has no friends," Geoffrey retorted scathingly. "He is reduced to gaming in the worst possible hells, because that is the only place they will let him play. And trust me, Mother, no one there will look out for him."

"Then he will lose a fortune," Lady Talbot said with calm resignation, "and come back much chastened. And for a while, perhaps a week or two or even a month he will swear off gaming. As he has so many times before. But you must not reduce your life to worrying about his."

She paused then added, "I never realized, until lately, when you went to salons with Lady Penelope and came back with such a spring in your step and your conversation filled with poets and science and all manner of things, just how great a disservice I did you when I called you home from the university to help me handle your father. I owe you an apology, Geoffrey."

Her voice broke as she said it and he was quick to catch up her hand in his. "No, Mama! I was happy to come and help. And who else should you have called upon?"

She shook her head. "What a bouncer," she said softly. "Happy? Never. You came, and I was glad for it. I knew you had all the qualities of honor your father does not. But that you were happy to leave the university? Don't even try to tell me such a lie.

"No, we both wronged you, your father and I. But at least I can begin to make up for it now. Go upstairs and dress. If you hurry you may still be able to find Lady Penelope at whatever ball she may be attending."

He hesitated. He started to say that Penelope didn't want to see him, but stopped. Because he found himself recalling so many things. Including how she had blossomed in his company. How he had blossomed in hers.

He would not let that be lost, that chance for happiness for both of them, because either he or she had too much pride. No, he would go to her and somehow, whatever it took, make her understand that despite all his mistakes, and hers, they were suited to each other.

Chapter 17

She saw him the moment he entered the room. Even before the murmurs reached her ears, naming the gentleman who was staring at her in such a blatant way.

He came straight toward her, the plump older man. People took care to step out of his way. "How de do," he said, bowing when he was close enough. "You're the Westcott chit, ain't you?"

He was very much the worse for wear and had clearly been indulging freely, either in port or something much stronger. His gaze was unsteady and he looked about to tip over at any moment.

Penelope looked helplessly to her mother who drew herself up to her full height and made to step between them. "I don't know who you are—" she began.

"Lord Talbot. M'son is the lad who got himself betrothed to this young lady. You are Lady Penelope, aren't you?" he asked, peering closer.

His father? Fascinated, Penelope nodded. "Is he here?" she managed to ask.

"Don't know where he is," Lord Talbot said airily. "But I heard you were here and thought I'd come around and pay my respects."

"You might have come to the house," Lady Westcott hissed. "You are creating a scene, my lord!"

He looked stricken and, in that moment, Penelope felt her heart go out to him. She, too, had landed herself in the briars, a time or two.

"It is quite all right," she said. "I am pleased to make your acquaintance."

"That's right. Prettily said, too," Lord Talbot told her approvingly.

Lady Westcott's face turned bright red with suppressed fury. Even Lady Brisbane found herself speechless. But Lord Talbot offered Penelope his arm and said, "Come take a turn about the room with this old fellow and tell me what this nonsense is about you crying off your betrothal with my son. He's deuced unhappy, I don't mind telling you. Told him it must be a misunderstanding. All nonsense. Easily cleared up. But he wouldn't believe me. So I came to ask you for the truth of it."

No doubt Mama or Aunt Ariana would have remonstrated had they thought there was any chance she would not send his lordship to the rightabout. But for once, Penelope did the unexpectedly demure thing. She smiled at Lord Talbot and took his arm.

Thus they were deep in conversation when Geoffrey Talbot set foot in the ballroom, a short time later.

Geoffrey's emotions were already in a quandary when he reached the Pontworth home. His mother's words echoed in his ears and he still feared where his father might be tonight. And then there was the question of what Lady Penelope would say when she saw him.

If she even spoke to him at all.

And if she did, how was he to explain why he had not tried to see her before tonight? Or why he had chosen such a public place. Geoffrey didn't have the slightest notion how he would answer her, either.

But all these concerns came to an abrupt halt as he stepped into the Pontworth ballroom and saw his father sitting on a sofa deep in conversation with Lady Penelope. And over on the other side of the room, Lady Westcott and Lady Brisbane looked to be in equally animated conversation. No doubt concerning the one between his father and Penelope, he thought grimly.

Several voices greeted Geoffrey and coyly asked if he was here to see his fiancée. From the way it was said he had no doubt someone had been talking. And the news of his quarrel with Lady Penelope had been spread far and wide.

One or two mothers tried to engage his attention so they could introduce him to their daughters. He ignored them and started toward his father and Lady Penelope, neither of whom had noticed him. Good. Then neither of them could try to flee.

"Well, isn't this a cozy sight," Geoffrey said sardonically, when he finally managed to reach the sofa where they were talking.

"Geoffrey, m'boy!" Lord Talbot said, rising to his feet.

"Mr. Talbot! What are you doing here?" Lady Penelope asked, looking at him wide-eyed, and coloring up most becomingly.

Geoffrey bowed to her and ignored his father. "Lady Penelope, surely you have not forgotten that we were pledged to dance every waltz together tonight."

She looked at him with eyes as haunted as his own. "You have already missed one," she whispered. Then, with a determined air, she added, "We were so pledged more than a week ago. You cannot mean to hold me to it still."

"Oh, but I do," he countered, just as softly.

He reached out, seized her hand, and pulled her with him, backward toward the dance floor. She meant to fight him, but there were too many interested eyes watching. She tilted up her chin defiantly.

For an instant, he told himself he ought to let her go. But then he saw something else. There was a hint of longing, a hint of relief in Lady Penelope's eyes that warmed Geoffrey and eased his guilt and gave him hope. And then they were whirling about, too swiftly for easy conversation. It

felt so good to hold her in his arms that Geoffrey found he
never wanted to let her go.

As for Lady Penelope, she leaned toward him, telling
herself that this would be the very last time she waltzed
with Mr. Talbot. And surely it could not hurt so very much
if she did so.

Geoffrey clasped her tighter.

Around and around the floor they went until Penelope
felt positively dizzy. As the last notes of the waltz died
away, he drew them up near her mother and aunt. And, he
realized with displeasure, his father.

Whatever antipathy the two older ladies might have felt
earlier for Lord Talbot had apparently been set aside. They
were smiling and laughing and inviting his lordship to call
on the morrow. Geoffrey felt something snap inside.

"It is time to go, Father," he said grimly.

Lord Talbot looked at him and lifted an eyebrow. "Indeed? I did not know you kept such early hours, son. Go
along home, if you must, but I mean to stay."

"You are the one who needs to leave," Geoffrey persisted.

Now Lord Talbot lost his air of easy amiability. In a
voice pitched low and meant only for his son to hear, he
said, "Not unless you mean to make a scene, and not likely,
even then. Recollect that I am your father, Geoffrey, not the
other way around."

He was right, of course, but that didn't make it any easier
for Talbot to accept. He clenched his fists by his side but
just stood there, trying to think of some discreet way to persuade his father to go.

And then he felt a gentle hand on his arm. He looked
down to see Penelope regarding him with concern in her
eyes. Once she saw that she had his attention, and his fists
unclenched, she turned to Lord Talbot.

"My dear sir," she said, "I am persuaded you must find
this sort of ball the most insipid thing imaginable."

"Well, of course I do," he agreed. "But mind, I don't grudge anything, if it's for the good of my son. Which coming here tonight was, you know."

"I do know it," Penelope persisted. "But you have done your good deed and, if you wanted to, you could leave now."

"You're trying to bamboozle me," Lord Talbot said shrewdly. "Mind, you're a good puss, but you ought to know it isn't going to work. Not when my son is treating me with such disrespect."

Penelope looked as if she could quite cheerfully strangle both father and son. Instead she persisted, saying coaxingly, "Well, I mean you no disrespect but I should think you would have far too much self-respect to stay at such a shabby event as this."

Lord Talbot touched his finger to the side of his nose. "I'll tell you what," he said. "I'll go if you come with me. Take me home, you can, and then Geoffrey can take you home. That's fair enough, ain't it?"

"No!" Geoffrey said, firmly. "For heaven's sake, Father, you don't know what you're asking. It would look very particular and draw unwanted attention to Lady Penelope."

Was that warmth in her eyes as she looked at him? Appreciation? Geoffrey was too busy to stop and try to tell. His father was going to be difficult.

"Then I'll make a scene," Lord Talbot said complacently.

"We can all go out at the same time," Lady Brisbane said sharply. "Right now, to be precise."

"Oh, yes, I have the headache and wish nothing more than to seek my bed," Lady Westcott fervently agreed.

Lord Talbot looked at each one in turn and then nodded. "Very well. We'll go out together. Propriety satisfied, and all that nonsense. And outside, Lady Penelope will ride with Geoffrey and me."

No argument, hastily whispered, could persuade him to alter his mind.

"We shall talk about this outside," Geoffrey said, taking his father by the arm.

Lord Talbot pulled his arm free. "Very bad *ton,* m'boy," he said reprovingly. "Offer your arm to your fiancée, and I'll offer mine to these lovely ladies."

There was nothing for it but to do as he said, or they would soon have the very scene he was trying to avoid. Outside, it took a few moments to arrange for the carriages to be brought around and when Geoffrey rejoined his father and the ladies, he found they had come to some sort of decision among them.

To his utter astonishment, Geoffrey found that both Lady Westcott and Lady Brisbane were willing to fall in with his father's truly outrageous plans. They intended to let Lady Penelope ride with the men.

"Absolutely not!" he sputtered.

Penelope, who had not been looking entirely pleased with the plan either, now altered her tune. She drew herself up straight and glared at him. Her eyes seemed to sparkle with anger as she rounded on him.

"How dare you presume to dictate what I may and may not do?" she demanded, advancing upon him.

Geoffrey, being a prudent man, hastily retreated. Penelope followed.

"I am not your wife. I am not even truly your fiancée. How dare you presume to decide anything for me? Dear God, I had begun to think myself mistaken in crying off from our betrothal! But you have just given me proof that I was right to cry off in the first place!"

Geoffrey was so startled at her words that he forgot to retreat any farther. He stopped so suddenly that Lady Penelope crashed right into him. Instinctively he reached out and caught and steadied her.

"You were beginning to regret your decision?" he asked, a foolish smile upon his face.

"You needn't look so pleased," she said crossly. "I have already regretted those regrets."

But he continued to stare down at her with that foolish smile upon his face and Penelope felt a warmth rising through her. It was all she could do to keep from rubbing her cheek against his chest and letting him wrap his arms around her.

Since that would never do, she pulled free and turned away, toward the others. Over her shoulder she said with cool impatience, "Well? Are you not coming? The carriages are here."

Bemused, bewildered, and greatly encouraged, Geoffrey followed and handed Lady Westcott and Lady Brisbane into their carriage.

"Now mind you bring her straight back to my house, once you have your father home," Lady Brisbane warned him sharply.

"Yes, and don't forget to use those moments alone to press your suit." Lady Westcott leaned forward to whisper in his ear. "My daughter has been missing you, you know."

Once they were settled, Geoffrey helped Lady Penelope and his father into his carriage. There he was most solicitous to both of them, asking if either would like a rug for their lap.

Lord Talbot snorted. "Don't need mollycoddling, m'boy. Never have, never will."

"I am fine, thank you," Penelope said almost shyly, a hint of a smile that she was trying very hard to suppress peeping out at him.

Geoffrey settled back, feeling much better than he had in days. He had not needed Lady Westcott's prodding to know that he must make use of every precious second alone with Lady Penelope to persuade her to let them continue their betrothal. He was so encouraged, in fact, that he might almost have whistled.

Except that he strongly suspected Lady Penelope would take exception to it and accuse him of arrogance and presumption. So, instead, Geoffrey settled a meek expression upon his face and spoke only polite nonsense as they drove the short distance home.

Once there he half expected his father to take off again, but to Geoffrey's surprise the old man went up the stairs to the house quite willingly, not needing the prodding Geoffrey was ready to give him. Instead, when the coach door was opened and Lord Talbot stood safely on the ground, he turned and looked his son directly in the eye.

"Don't waste this chance, m'boy. I've done my best to pave the way for you, but it's in your hands now. She's a nice gel, she'll suit you right down to the ground. Don't let her get away."

Touched, despite himself, by his father's patent concern, Geoffrey answered gently, "I don't mean to. And thank you."

Lord Talbot was startled. "Eh? What for?" he asked suspiciously.

"For caring. For wishing to help."

Now it was Lord Talbot's turn to smile and for once Geoffrey saw a little of that famous charm which had made his lordship such a popular member of society so many years ago. And for the first time in far too long, he could begin to understand why his mother had married the man.

And then Lord Talbot was inside and Geoffrey was heading back down the steps to the carriage. The question was, how best to use his few moments alone with Lady Penelope?

It did not help that when he climbed back inside, Geoffrey found Lady Penelope had moved herself to the farthest corner of the carriage, crossed her arms over her chest, and was glaring at him.

"Don't think to turn me up sweet," she warned. "Nothing you can say can excuse what you did."

"You're right," he said meekly.

"You were horrid."

"So I was."

"You made me think quite ridiculous things about you," she persisted crossly.

"It was the only way to not have you turn me away completely," he countered coaxingly.

"You cannot have wanted my company that badly."

Was there a lessening of the anger in her voice? A hint that she was not quite as inexorably set against him as she said?

Geoffrey moved to sit beside, rather than opposite Lady Penelope.

"Oh, but I did," he assured her, taking her hand in his.

She pulled it free. "I was probably the subject of endless wagers at White's," she said with a disapproving sniff.

"You were the subject of endless dreams in my heart," he replied.

She looked at him then, her eyes wide, wanting to believe. "Truly?" she asked, her voice catching on that one word.

He nodded. And then, before she could recollect her anger or turn away again, he drew her gently into his arms, giving her time to refuse if she truly wished. He held his breath, but to his delight, she didn't draw back.

And when he dipped his head to kiss her, she lifted her chin to offer up her lips. In that moment, Geoffrey knew everything was going to be all right, after all. He could not hide the triumphant gleam in his eyes. And that was his mistake.

Chapter 18

Penelope saw the gleam in Mr. Talbot's eyes and knew it for what it was. She drew back and pushed him away, hastily moving toward the corner of the carriage.

"No! You are not going to come over me like that," she said, pursing up her lips in anger.

"Why not?" he asked, puzzled.

He reached out to stroke the side of her cheek. Penelope jerked her head away. "Because we are going to talk about this like sensible people," she said firmly.

He hesitated. "What did my father say to you?" Mr. Talbot asked, suspicion strong in his voice.

Penelope gave a short, sharp laugh. "He told me I should think myself lucky to be betrothed to you and tried to tell me any faults in your character were due to him and I might remedy them quite easily once we were wed."

"And did you believe him?"

There was longing and uncertainty and something oddly touching in his voice. Penelope tried to steel herself against it. She reminded herself of every reason she had to resist his charm. She remembered the rumors she had heard tonight about his father.

"Given that I must assume your mother tried to reform Lord Talbot," she said in withering accents, "I cannot see any reason to believe that I would have better luck with you."

Mr. Talbot slumped back against the cushions. "Blast my father!" he muttered angrily. "He has done nothing but cause trouble since before the day I was born."

Was that how it had been for him? Then at least some of the rumors must be true. But Penelope could not conceive that it could truly have been so bad. She reached across the space between them and touched Mr. Talbot's hand.

When he looked at her mutinously, she said gently, "I collect your father has been a sad trial to you and I can very well see why. But you are doing as much harm to yourself as he ever could."

"The devil I am!" he said angrily. "You do not know the half of it."

"Whatever the truth," she said gravely, "you are still hurting yourself."

Now it was his turn to glare and, after a moment, she said, "Why did you never tell me about him? I thought we were friends."

"Do you think I am proud of him?" Mr. Talbot demanded, meeting her eyes defiantly. "Do you think I wish my friends to know what sort of man he is?"

"Do you think we would think any less of you, if you did?" Penelope countered gently. "I cannot speak for your other friends, but I would not have done so."

He had no answer for her. When it was clear he did not mean to speak, she went on: "You want to deny him. But in doing so, you are denying a part of yourself. There must have been a time you looked up to him, times when he made you laugh or smile."

"If there were, I cannot recall a single one," Mr. Talbot said shortly.

Penelope's smile took on an edge of sadness. She found she had the oddest wish to hold Mr. Talbot in her arms and make his unhappiness disappear.

Instead she said, "Then to deny the sadness he brought to you and your mother is to deny much of what made you who you are. It is to deny the trials that forged your character and made you someone I admire."

Mr. Talbot looked at her and his smile was derisive, but whether to her or to himself she could not tell. "Do you admire me?" he countered. "I thought you held me in contempt."

It was her turn to feel confusion. She tried to choose her words with utmost care. "I was—I am—angry that you lied to me. That you deceived me from the start. But yes, I do admire your mind. Your kindness. Oh, I don't know, any number of things!"

Once again Geoffrey shifted seats. Again she moved away. He moved closer. He took her hand in his. He kissed her fingertips.

"Do you not think that perhaps there is a chance we could continue our betrothal?" he asked meekly, as he kissed her wrist. "I would try very hard to be the fiancé you wished me to be."

Her voice was so low he could scarcely hear it as she said, "Perhaps."

Penelope drew in her breath. She did not give herself time to think. Before she could let any notions of propriety stop her, she reached up and touched his face. And then she tried to kiss him.

It was a clumsy effort. She ought to have known better. The next thing she knew, she had overset both of them and they almost tumbled off the seat of the coach and onto the floor.

But Mr. Talbot caught her. He steadied them both and then, drawing in his own breath, he bent his head and kissed her. Gently, thoroughly, and in a way that captured her heart, despite everything.

Was that a tiny moan? It came from the back of her own throat. And it was she who clung to him even more tightly than he held her clasped to his breast.

He feathered kisses on her cheeks, her eyelids, even nibbled on her ear. He captured her lips and toyed with them until she parted her own to give him the entrance he now demanded.

But abruptly the coach came to a halt and she pulled away at precisely the same moment he did. Her breath and his both came in gasps and it took every shred of self-control Penelope possessed to bring hers under control again.

Apparently Mr. Talbot did so as well, for when the coach door opened, he sprang down and handed her out with a coolness she could not have managed.

At least Penelope hoped he was far from feeling as calm as he appeared. It would not be fair if she were the only one who had been touched by what had passed between them.

Geoffrey was far from feeling calm or untouched. Indeed, it was all he could do not to crow with delight. But he was afraid Lady Penelope would turn her back on him in anger if he did so.

He was also afraid that if he did not let her go inside, she might start talking about his father again. And there were so many things he could not bring himself to tell her. It was admirable that she had a kind heart toward the fellow, but he did not know what he would do if she asked him again to share it.

She thought she understood, but she didn't. And Geoffrey couldn't help thinking it was better that way. Better for her and better for him.

"I shall see you tomorrow," was all he said, in as grave a tone as he could manage.

Inside, Penelope found everyone waiting for her in the drawing room. Her mother and Aunt Ariana were pacing restlessly and her father was looking harried.

"Well?" they cried as one when she came into the room.

Penelope was too tired to dissemble. She sank into the nearest chair and said, "Well, we have agreed, for the moment, to continue our betrothal."

Lady Westcott flew to her daughter's side and hugged Penelope. "I knew it would all come about!" she said brightly.

"Well! I am glad to see you are finally showing some sense," Lady Brisbane said sardonically. "I only hope you continue to do so."

Only Lord Westcott seemed perturbed. "Are you quite certain this is what you wish, Penelope?"

Both she and her father ignored the cries of protest from her mother and aunt. Penelope looked directly at her father as she nodded slowly.

"Yes, Papa, I think it is."

Now he smiled and heaved himself to his feet. "In that case," he declared, "I am off to bed."

Lady Brisbane and Lady Westcott would have crowded around Penelope and demanded details of the reconciliation but one glance at her face and they decided that perhaps it would be wisest to follow Lord Westcott's course.

"Yes, dearest, it is late. Perhaps we should all seek our beds," Lady Westcott said.

"I confess I am tired," Lady Brisbane said with a yawn. "We may talk again in the morning, after all."

And so, in a few short minutes, Penelope found herself alone in her room, in her night rail, the maid sent off to bed herself.

She sat by the window and rested her forehead against the glass as she looked out at the night. Had she made a fatal error tonight? And if she had not, what would she do when it came to the point of actually marrying Mr. Talbot or crying off?

"Geoffrey," she whispered softly to the moonlight.

Penelope could no longer imagine a lifetime without Mr. Talbot. And yet neither could she see herself a wife. She did not think Mr. Talbot would become like his father and yet what if he had other vices? Vices she would have no more power to control than Lady Talbot apparently did her husband's?

It was a frightening thought, and not for the first time Penelope wished her twin were still here. But Rebecca was long gone back to the north of London and this was a decision Penelope would have to make all alone.

Well, not quite all alone, she admitted. Indeed, it would be easier if there were not so many interested persons wishing to advise her. The trouble was, she trusted none of them, except perhaps Miss Tibbles. And for the past several days, she had been most unaccountably silent.

A soft rap on the bedroom door startled Penelope and she hastened to open it. There in the hallway stood Miss Tibbles, candle in hand, hair braided down the back of her neck. To her surprise, Penelope realized Miss Tibbles looked quite young.

"I—I was just thinking of you," Penelope stammered.

The governess lifted her eyebrows inquiringly but did not ask the obvious question aloud. Instead she asked, "May I come in?"

"Of course."

Penelope opened the door wider to let Miss Tibbles enter. The governess set her candle down on the small table beside the bed and then sat down.

"Your mother woke me to say that you have decided to continue your betrothal after all," she said.

Penelope looked everywhere but at Miss Tibbles. And yet, wasn't this just what she had been wishing she could talk about with her?

"Yes, we did. But only for the moment," Penelope finally told her.

"I see."

The governess fell silent and Penelope wondered what she was thinking of. She did not think it would be a good idea to ask her. If Miss Tibbles wished her to know, Miss Tibbles would tell her.

When the silence had stretched on far too long, Penelope asked timidly, "Do you approve or disapprove?"

"Me?" Miss Tibbles looked startled. "It is not my place to do either."

"But you do," Penelope countered shrewdly.

Miss Tibbles hesitated, then nodded. "Yes, I do," she said briskly. "But I should rather know how you feel about your decision. Were you pressed to it? Or did it come from your heart?"

Miss Tibbles certainly had a way of getting straight to the point of the matter. Penelope sank down onto the bed beside the governess.

"My heart," she admitted reluctantly.

"And that is what frightens you most?" Miss Tibbles hazarded.

"How did you know?"

Miss Tibbles gave a sigh of exasperation. "After the past few years with this family, how could I not know how you would feel?" she demanded. "You are terrified. If it were a marriage of convenience you might be defiant. You might acquiesce, though I have trouble imagining you doing so. But if your heart is engaged, then you fear to lose yourself."

"Precisely!" Penelope looked at Miss Tibbles with a woebegone expression on her face. "How can I know I will not?" she asked.

Miss Tibbles sighed softly. "That is the trouble, my dear," she said, "you cannot."

Penelope gave a tiny cry of dismay and Miss Tibbles immediately said, far more briskly, "But I do not think you will. Consider! In all your years, has your family ever been able to make you do something you did not wish to do?"

"They made me come to London. They made me have a Season. Two, in fact!"

Miss Tibbles shook her head. "Trivialities. When it matters most, you hold your own very well, Penelope. I imagine you will do the same after you are married. If I did not think he deserved you, I should almost pity Mr. Talbot."

And then, before Penelope could take offense or object to this statement, Miss Tibbles was on her feet and moving toward the door.

"Good night, my dear. And do try not to worry. It will all come about you know."

The door closed behind the diminutive governess.

Was she right? Penelope asked herself as she climbed into bed. If only Rebecca were here to ask! As she lay in the dark, a plan began to form in her mind. What if she went to visit her sister? Surely no one could object to that?

And while she was away, Penelope told herself, she would surely be able to think more clearly, her mind unclouded by the way she felt when Mr. Talbot touched her hand or, heaven forbid, kissed her!

The fact that he had gone beyond the line ought to have shocked Penelope. It ought to have sent her running to her parents to cry for their help in putting Mr. Talbot in his place.

Instead, it caused her to fall asleep with Geoffrey's name on her tongue, even though she could not bring herself to call him so to his face. And when she dreamed of him, he was as bold or bolder than before, and she threw to the winds every precept of her training. Propriety, in her dreams at least, did not stand between them.

She woke in the early hours of the morning from just such a dream, her heart pounding. She could not stay here, Penelope thought, and marry Mr. Talbot. Not if he could turn her thoughts so far astray. Barbara's reassurances to the contrary, she could not bear the thought that anyone, particularly any man, could have so profound an effect upon her nature.

She must, she thought, even as she tried to go back to sleep, find a way to see Rebecca!

Chapter 19

Geoffrey Talbot's euphoria over having, at least partially, retrieved his position with Lady Penelope suffered a severe setback when he returned home. There he discovered that his father had once again gone out. And this time he did not return.

It was morning before either Geoffrey or his mother saw Lord Talbot again. They were sitting at the breakfast table, carefully not speaking of the person foremost on their minds. Instead, Geoffrey tried to divert his mother's thoughts by mentioning his renewed betrothal.

Lady Talbot was not as pleased as one might have expected. She set her teacup down with a snap and said, frowning, "I hope that this time you mean to be honest with Lady Penelope. And that you are genuinely fond of her."

"I am, Mama," he said, taken aback.

He would have gone on to assure her more, but at that moment there was a rapping at the front door. Lady Talbot and Geoffrey looked at one another.

"Who could be calling at this hour?" she wondered aloud.

The question was quickly answered when both Lord Talbot and Frederick Baines were ushered into the dining room. Grimly Geoffrey wondered what the latest disaster might entail. He noted that his father looked very much the worse for wear, but Baines looked as fresh as if he had just dressed for the day.

"My apologies for disturbing you," Baines said, bowing to both Geoffrey and Lady Talbot. "But I thought it best to personally escort Lord Talbot home. Mr. Talbot, if I might have a word with you in private?"

"Of course. This way."

Geoffrey left his father to his mother's care. As he left the dining room, he could hear her coaxing his father to be seated and asking if he wished some tea.

He led Frederick Baines to the study and there faced him, wondering what on earth the man could want. Baines came quickly to the point. He dropped a pile of small pieces of paper on the desk before Geoffrey.

"These are your father's vowels. To the tune of several thousand pounds, I believe."

Geoffrey went very white. "I shall redeem them, of course. It may take me a few days to draw the funds."

Baines shook his head. "You mistake me, Talbot. I am returning them and telling you they can be ripped up and thrown away."

Geoffrey stared at the pile of vowels. Through gritted teeth he said, "We Talbots pay our debts."

"Admirable," Baines agreed calmly. "Save that we are about to become family, you and I. And while I understand perfectly that you may dislike me, I will not take money from family."

He wanted to refuse. He wanted to be able to laugh and insist. Instead Geoffrey smiled bitterly. "You are very good to us. And very optimistic concerning Lady Penelope and her feelings toward me. Still, I thank you. For this and for bringing my father home." He paused and then made himself ask, "Where was he?"

Frederick told him. "I think he means to leave London," he added blandly.

Geoffrey looked at the man sharply. "Now how did you accomplish that?" he asked.

Baines shrugged. "A word or two, dropped in his ear. You might let him stay, however, until after your wedding. I do not think he will disgrace you before then."

"Is there to be a wedding? I am not nearly so certain," Geoffrey said wryly. "Has Lady Penelope told you something she has not told me?"

"Me? Why, no. But I have eyes in my head. So she is still angry? Pity. I had thought you must have turned her up sweet by now. Ah, well. You will."

"And will you be staying for the wedding?" Geoffrey could not help but ask.

Baines hesitated and, for the first time, his air of self-assurance left him. There was a hint, but only a hint, of bitterness in his voice as he said quietly, "No. Shan't do that. The family would never forgive me if I did. They don't speak of me, you know. Or see me, if they can avoid it. I shan't spoil Penelope's wedding day."

Abruptly Geoffrey came over and held out his hand to Frederick Baines. "Most assuredly you will spoil it if you are not there," he said quietly but firmly.

Frederick looked at the hand held out to him and slowly took it. Then he smiled and it was a singularly sweet smile. "She is getting a damn fine man," he said, "and so I told her. But I think I'll tell her again."

And then Baines was gone, taking his leave despite Geoffrey's efforts to persuade him to sit down to breakfast with them. Talbot swept the pieces of paper into his pocket, knowing that later he would look at them and add the totals in his head. He needed to know how deeply his father had been playing.

He also knew, with a part of himself he did not admire, that he would save these vowels. So that if ever his father behaved this badly again, he would have something to hold over his father's head. It was a measure of his desperation, his despair of years of helplessness where his father was concerned, that Geoffrey could even contemplate doing such a thing.

In the dining room, he found Lord Talbot looking distinctly more sober. He was sipping coffee and eating toast. As Geoffrey came into the room, he looked up at him and flinched.

In that moment, Talbot knew he did not have the heart to ring a peal over his father's head. His mother looked at him questioningly.

"Has he gone?" she asked.

"Mr. Baines? Yes. He wished to assure me there will be no ill consequences from last night," Geoffrey said to her.

"But there might have been?"

"Yes, there might have been," Geoffrey agreed. "I have the proof in my pocket."

Lady Talbot bit her lower lip. Lord Talbot looked from one to the other. When he spoke, he startled both of them.

"It's over, you know. I shan't game anymore. Not even for penny a point."

Lady Talbot looked everywhere but at her husband's face. Geoffrey snorted.

"You don't believe me," Lord Talbot said quietly, "but I mean it."

Now Lady Talbot did look at him. "You've said that before."

Lord Talbot nodded. "So I have. And you won't believe me until enough time has passed to prove it true."

"Why?" Geoffrey asked. "Why change your tune now?"

Lord Talbot's hand shook so much his cup rattled against the saucer as he set it down. "Because," he said, "I've come to see how badly I've hurt the pair of you."

He paused and took a breath.

"For a long time I told myself it didn't matter. That Lydia wanted to marry someone else, anyway. And that you were an unfeeling, ungrateful son. So I owed neither of you anything."

He looked at Geoffrey. "I know I've railed that a fortune came to you when I could have used it. But it has been pointed out to me that if it were not for you, working so hard to salvage the estate these past few years, I should have lost everything long ago."

Now Lord Talbot looked at Lady Talbot. "And you, my dear. It has been pointed out to me that you married me out of love and have been loyal to me ever since, despite far too much provocation to do otherwise. You have never played me false. All the error, in that respect, has been mine and I am sorry for it."

She wanted to hold herself proof against him. But the gentle, sad way he looked at her was her undoing. Slowly, against her will, she let herself reach out and touch his hand. Instantly he clasped it tightly and brought it to his lips. The kiss was both promise and apology and despite herself, and against all common sense, Lady Talbot found that she trusted both.

Geoffrey didn't want to trust, didn't want to believe his father either. There had been too many years of lies. Too many years of hurt.

Lord Talbot must have guessed what he was feeling, for he said, "I don't ask you to trust or believe me right this moment, Geoffrey. I just ask that you watch and see whether I have truly changed. And understand that for all my flaws, I am proud of the man you have become. A far better man than I shall ever be."

He looked from one to the other, then asked his son, "Shall I go and pack? I shan't object if you send me back home today."

Lady Talbot looked at Geoffrey. He wanted to tell his father, in words as cutting as he could make them, that, yes, he would be in the traveling coach, on his way home, before noon. Instead, with Frederick Baines's words echoing in his ears, he shook his head.

"No, you need not go today. Perhaps, if I can persuade

Lady Penelope to set a date, you could even stay for the wedding."

Geoffrey could not bear to see the poignant looks on both his parents' faces so he fled the room, saying over his shoulder, "I think I had better go and call upon Lady Penelope."

They let him go.

At Lady Brisbane's household, he found another surprise. He met Frederick Baines coming down the steps even as he went up them.

"You'll find her ambivalent," Baines told him with an amused chuckle. "But I daresay you can bring her around. If you can remember that she is your equal and not someone you can order about."

Geoffrey nodded, not trusting himself to speak. Did the man have a finger in every pie?

The footman would have told Talbot that it was too early to call, but Jeffries, the majordomo, recognized the niceties that might allow for an exception in this case. He showed Talbot into the drawing room.

"If you will wait, sir, I am certain Lady Penelope will see you shortly."

"Whenever she is ready," Geoffrey said with an air of carelessness he did not feel.

In point of fact, Talbot was rather grateful for the reprieve. Had he been asked, he could not have said why he had come here. Certainly it was not a proper hour for him to do so. The temporary truce he had forged with Lady Penelope the night before was a fragile one and he might well shatter it by such behavior.

Nor would it be proper for him to speak to her of his father, even if Geoffrey could have brought himself to do so. At any rate, not of the proclivities which distressed him most. But he had found himself coming here anyway.

And what precisely that meant, he refused to contemplate. Instead he all but wore a path in the carpet, pacing about the room as he waited for Lady Penelope.

Penelope hesitated in the hallway. When Jeffries, the majordomo, informed her that Mr. Talbot was in the drawing room, Penelope was tempted to ask him to say she was not at home. She had just had a most trying interview with her uncle, who had pressed Mr. Talbot's suit for him. It had settled nothing. She still did not understand her own feelings for Mr. Talbot and the last thing she wanted was to be pressed on the point again. And after last night, she scarcely trusted herself or him.

But she would see Mr. Talbot, Penelope decided at last. She would see him and make it very clear that even though she had agreed to continue the betrothal, she would not have him living in her pocket, nor would she live in his.

So with the words rehearsed in her mind and her face set in cool, distant lines, Penelope opened the door to the drawing room. She noted with satisfaction that he had evidently been pacing while waiting for her. So perhaps he was not as certain of himself as he seemed.

Then he turned. And all her plans to ring a peal over his head were forgotten. There was such a look of woebegone unhappiness there, Penelope found herself moving across the room to him, her arms held wide open.

Mr. Talbot came into them and for several moments they embraced silently. He did not try to kiss her, nor explain a thing. He only clung to her as if he feared he would drown without her.

It was, Penelope discovered, a very pleasant feeling, to be needed like this. Still, she was almost afraid to ask what was wrong, afraid he would retreat behind the polite facade she knew so well. Afraid they would both retreat to the propriety that she had once thought an inescapable part of her.

So she clung to him and hoped that, in due course, he would tell her what was wrong. He did not. Just as she thought he must crush all feelings out of her, he let her go and drew her to sit beside him on the sofa. And when he did speak, his words were not at all what she expected.

"Shall we set a date for our wedding?" he asked briskly.

Penelope stared at Mr. Talbot. "Do you not wish to talk about whatever it is that has distressed you?"

He looked at her with an expression she often saw in her mother and father's face when she asked something they considered an impertinence.

"I can see no need to do so," he said, tilting up his chin.

"No need?" Penelope echoed indignantly. "But when I came in, I saw how distressed you were."

"And now I am better and wish to forget the matter," Mr. Talbot answered. "Come, it is time we set a date for our wedding. Both my family and yours will need to make plans and arrangements. There is a great deal to be done, I collect, for these sorts of things."

Again she echoed him. "These sorts of things."

Abruptly Penelope rose to her feet and began to walk about the room. She saw that Mr. Talbot was watching her with a faintly puzzled look upon his face and she found that she had a strong desire to box his ears.

When she had worked herself to a high degree of emotion, and he had begun to show signs of impatience, Penelope turned to Mr. Talbot and said, "I do not think I can set a date to marry you. Indeed, I am not certain I wish to marry you at all."

He looked thunderstruck. "But—but you said . . . last night . . ."

She stood still as she answered him. "Last night I thought we could make a match of it. Today I see how great the gulf is between us. You would brush everything under the carpet, as my family has always done. And I know it is supposed to be so. But I cannot bear the notion. If I am to be married at all, it must be to someone who can enter into my sentiments. To someone who can trust me enough to share with me all that he feels, all that is of importance to him. You will not do so. Very well, I shall remain a spinster. For the rest of my life. It will not, I assure you, be a very grave hardship. Better that than a marriage which can only hold unhappiness for the both of us!"

A stricken look crossed Mr. Talbot's face and he rose to his feet, starting to hold out one hand to her. Before she could weaken, before he could touch her and destroy all her resolve in so doing, Penelope whirled on her heel and all but ran from the room. Behind her, she could hear him calling her name. She ignored it and only ran faster.

On the stairs, halfway up, she encountered Miss Tibbles. The governess took one look at Penelope's face and said with patent dismay, "Oh, dear! You have not patched it up, after all, have you?"

Penelope halted long enough to swallow and reply, "No, Miss Tibbles. And I think we never shall."

"Oh, dear," the governess repeated. "What do you mean to do?"

"What I should have done at the first," Penelope retorted. "I shall go and stay with Rebecca. She will understand!"

Then, before Miss Tibbles could object, or anyone else appear, Penelope fled the rest of the way to her room. There, with the door safely closed, she dissolved into the worst bout of tears she could ever recall.

No one, she vowed fiercely, was ever going to persuade her to agree to anything ever again!

In the hallway, a very stunned Miss Tibbles stood clinging to the railing.

"I don't think Lord and Lady Westcott are going to like

this idea," she said softly to herself. "I am very much afraid they are not going to like it at all."

Unfortunately, she had not the slightest notion what to do to alter the matter. And given the expression on Penelope's face, Miss Tibbles was not at all sure she wished to try.

Chapter 20

Miss Tibbles was right. Lord and Lady Westcott did not like the notion of Penelope leaving London, particularly when matters were at such a stand with Mr. Talbot. But in the end they had to let her go.

It was much the wisest choice, they finally agreed, to allow Penelope to visit her sister. So long as she insisted that she was unalterably opposed to marriage with Mr. Talbot, it was preferable not to expose her to the tattle-mongers of the *ton*. Or their patent censure.

Perhaps the sight of Rebecca so happily married would have a salutary effect on Penelope's attitude toward marriage. That was what Lord and Lady Westcott told themselves. Their one stipulation was that no notice should be sent to the papers announcing the betrothal had been broken off until after she returned. It was the Westcott's devout hope that by then Penelope would have come to her senses!

Lord Westcott's coachman drove Penelope and Miss Tibbles north not two days after her argument with Mr. Talbot. And although the coach was very well sprung, it was a journey none of them found very comfortable.

There had been no time to send word to Rebecca. Penelope was certain her twin would understand and yet she could not help but fret that Rebecca would be unhappy to have her arrive unannounced on her doorstep.

As for Miss Tibbles, she still felt the sting of reproof from Lord and Lady Westcott that she had not managed their daughter better. And the poor coachman was forced to drive along dusty roads, in unpleasant weather, and more than once, for several hours in the rain. Nor were the poor outriders in any better case. But they went on.

Penelope could not shake the fear that Mr. Talbot might follow them. It was a foolish fear, perhaps. What gentleman would choose to make a laughingstock of himself in such a way? That was what she told herself, and yet she could not shake the fear.

They arrived, finally, in the early afternoon of the third day, exhausted. Penelope and Miss Tibbles looked at one another.

"Come along," the diminutive governess said after a moment. "We are rude enough as it is, arriving like this, unannounced. We are not going to make matters any worse by forcing them to come out to greet us."

And with that she fixed such a minatory gleam on Penelope that she sighed and promptly jumped down from the coach. It was true there was no point in putting matters off. She had wanted to come north and she had.

Already the front door stood open, their arrival having been sighted, apparently, by someone in the house, and Rebecca was hurrying down the steps. Immediately Penelope rushed toward her and threw herself in her sister's arms.

Mr. Rowland, Rebecca's husband, stood watching bemused, as his steward gave orders to the coachman and outriders as to how to find the stables. He looked at Miss Tibbles and lifted his brows in a questioning way. She merely shrugged and grimaced her own confusion.

"I hope you do not think it too rude of me to arrive like this, unannounced," Penelope said at last, a patent note of uncertainty in her voice.

"Of course not, silly goose!" Rebecca replied, giving her sister an affectionate shake. "Come in and I shall have rooms prepared for you at once. And Miss Tibbles! How pleased I am to see you again. How are you? I do hope the journey was not too uncomfortable for you?"

As Miss Tibbles was about to answer, a swarm of children suddenly appeared from around the side of the house and surrounded both Miss Tibbles and Penelope.

"Who are all these children?" Miss Tibbles asked Rebecca faintly.

She hesitated and it was Mr. Rowland who answered, a mischievous glint in his eyes as he said, "Ours."

For a moment, both Penelope and Miss Tibbles gaped at Rebecca and Hugh in disbelief. Then the governess snapped her mouth shut and said, "Do not speak such nonsense to me! They cannot all be your children. I collect you have set up some sort of school here?"

It was Hugh Rowland's turn to hesitate and Rebecca's to answer. "More than a school, Miss Tibbles," she said. "We have brought most of these children from London where they were living on the streets, with no homes or parents to turn to for care. In a very real sense they are our children and always will be."

And then, to Miss Tibbles's way of thinking, the most incredible thing of all happened. Penelope dropped to her knees and grinned at several of the nearest children. She even swept two little girls into a grand hug.

"Well, if they are your children," she said softly, "then I suppose we must all learn to love them!"

In all her eight and thirty years of life, Miss Tibbles had never fainted. The notion was preposterous. And yet, in that moment, she came very, very close. So concerned was she with not disgracing herself that she did not see the look which passed between Penelope and her sister.

But Rebecca understood perfectly. "Come along with me, Penelope," she said brightly. "We shall have a comfortable coze and it shall be just as it always was. Hugh shall attend to everything here."

With a brief twinge of guilt, Penelope left Miss Tibbles surrounded by children. She had never seen her governess with such a bewildered air. Good. It would keep her from following too soon and overhearing too much. Penelope loved her dearly, but there was no question Miss Tibbles was on the side of marriage.

"Now," Rebecca said, the moment they were alone, "tell me everything! I cannot believe you have broken your vow never to marry. I should be very happy if I truly thought it was what you wished, but surely it cannot be so?"

Penelope suddenly found that she could not meet her sister's eyes. "Surely you have had my letters?" she countered.

"Yes, and they have been strangely lacking in the very details I have most wished to know," Rebecca retorted dryly. "Had you not come to visit me, I must have come to London to discover the truth for myself."

Penelope hesitated. She twisted her hands together. She looked at the floor. She considered walking over to the window and pretending to admire the view. But Rebecca was her sister, her twin, and they had been far too close, all their lives, for such an evasion now.

Penelope drew in her breath. "Oh, Rebecca, I have not known what to write! Or how to tell you what I do not understand myself."

"Begin with your betrothal," Rebecca suggested gently. "I know there must be a great deal more to it than you have said in your letters."

"He, Mr. Talbot, seemed to wish for marriage no more than I," Penelope said. "It was his notion to pretend. Too late I discovered it was no pretense. He meant to marry me from the very first."

Rebecca laughed. She did not wish to do so, but she could scarcely help herself.

"Why ever should you have believed him?" she gasped.

Penelope felt her lips press into a tight line and she was

helpless to prevent it. "I thought he was like Uncle Frederick," she said.

"Oh."

That one word, spoken softly, held so much meaning.

Penelope drew in a deep breath and went on, "How could I explain that I had begun to care so deeply for a man who could not, I believed, care for me."

"Is that why you are here?" Rebecca asked gravely.

Penelope shook her head. "No, I am here because I have discovered that Mr. Talbot is not like Uncle Frederick, after all."

"Ah. So you have broken off your betrothal?" Rebecca hazarded shrewdly.

Again Penelope shook her head, but with much less certainty this time. "I have said that I wish to do so, but Mama and Papa insisted I wait until after my visit to you. If Mr. Talbot would only talk frankly with me—but he will not, and I do not know what to do."

Rebecca regarded her sister with grim frustration. "If you do not tell me every little detail that is pertinent to what is going on, this very moment, I vow I shall shake you!" she said.

Now Penelope did meet Rebecca's eyes and there was perplexed misery in her own.

"Rebecca," she said, "I think I am in love with Mr. Talbot!"

Lady Westcott would have cried with joy. Lord Westcott would have pronounced the matter nicely settled. Rebecca promptly sat in the nearest chair and exclaimed, "Oh, dear."

"Precisely," Penelope said, drawing courage from Rebecca's instant comprehension. "It would be different if he were different. If we had come to the right sort of understanding between us. If either we both had lost our hearts to one another or neither of us. If he could see me as a partner in marriage and not a wife."

Rebecca did not argue. She understood her twin too well. Soon Penelope found herself telling everything that had happened since the moment she met Mr. Talbot.

When Penelope was done, her sister took a deep breath and said, "It was not well done of him. Indeed it sounds almost unpardonable. But I wonder if he feels more for you than you suspect."

Penelope could only stare at her sister unhappily. "Whether he does or does not, how can I marry a man who will not be honest with me?"

"What do you mean to do?" Rebecca asked.

Penelope took a turn around the room before she came to a halt in front of her twin.

"I don't know!" she said, her forehead wrinkled with dismay. "There is much to like about Mr. Talbot. And in so many ways we are suited. But still, I cannot bring myself to put my self, my future, into his hands. And yet, when he is near, I find that all my resolve to send him to the rightabout washes away and I do not know which would be the greater folly."

"Never mind," Rebecca said soothingly. "You may have all the time you need to consider the matter. I shan't press you to come to the point before you are ready."

Penelope smiled gratefully at her sister and shook her head. "Not you, but Mama and Papa and Aunt Ariana will. They are already dismayed by my indecision and have cut up rough over it. They trust this visit to set my mind to rights so that I shall marry Mr. Talbot after all, and soon."

"What about Miss Tibbles? What does she say?" Rebecca asked thoughtfully.

That prompted an unexpected laugh from Penelope. "Miss Tibbles is scarcely speaking to me," she said. "She is dreadfully annoyed at being dragged this far north. Indeed," she added, "I daresay it would be a wise notion to return to her before I have entirely sunk myself beneath reproach with her."

With a devilishly mischievous grin on each of their faces, Rebecca and Penelope linked arms. As they walked back to the foyer, Rebecca told her twin, "We shall talk more about your Mr. Talbot later. For now you must put him out of your mind and simply be happy you are here with me."

In the foyer they found Mr. Rowland looking far too eager for rescue and Miss Tibbles under siege by several urchins. The look of dismay on the governess's face was comically desperate.

At the sight of them, Miss Tibbles grimaced. Tartly she said, "Why ever do you not control these children better, Rebecca?"

How her sister could answer without betraying the least smile was more than Penelope could comprehend. It was all she could do not to burst out laughing.

"I thought, perhaps, you could take a hand while you are here," Rebecca said demurely.

Miss Tibbles's eyes flashed with something very close to rage. And desperation. She drew herself up to every inch of her diminutive height and said imperiously, "That is not my duty."

"There, there," Penelope said, patting Miss Tibbles on the shoulder. "Rebecca is only roasting you."

"Oh, no, I am quite serious," Rebecca retorted unrepentantly. "Why look at the excellent job she did with us."

Still, Rebecca did turn to Mr. Rowland and say to him, "If you will shepherd the children back to their wing of the house, Hugh, I shall take my sister and Miss Tibbles up to their rooms."

He nodded and smiled amiably and with a word and a crook of his finger, drew the children all to himself. Even as he disappeared down the hallway with them, his voice trailed back to the ladies as he explained how they had traveled to here from London and how long it took and by what other means they might have done so.

He looked for all the world like the proud father of all these children, and Penelope watched with a wistful envy the look of love that gentled and transfigured her sister's face. Would it really be so horrible, she wondered, to feel that way herself about a man?

Yes, she answered silently. If he were a liar who could not tell her the truth, it would be horrible to love him. She would always find herself trying to believe his lies. She looked over and caught Miss Tibbles watching her, a sympathetic, understanding look upon the woman's face.

Because all these thoughts were far more than she could bear, Penelope turned to her sister and said sharply, "Well, Rebecca? Do you mean to show us to our rooms or not?"

And blast Rebecca! She wore just such an understanding smile as Miss Tibbles. But pity was one emotion Penelope did not wish to see anymore.

Chapter 21

Geoffrey Talbot cursed and muttered and kicked the damaged wheel of his phaeton. He ought to have stayed, that day, and talked with Lady Penelope further. He ought never to have walked away as he had.

But what good would it have done, when he could not bring himself to answer her questions? But if he had been able to do so, he would not now be in such a mess.

And it was a mess, indeed. For all his vaunted rejection of the notion of love, Geoffrey had become most exquisitely aware, over the past few days, that he had fallen prey to the malady. Sensible or not, he had discovered that Lady Penelope had become inexplicably necessary to him, inexplicably important to his heart.

But instead of being in London, pleading his case with her, he now stood by the side of the road, covered with mud, while his valet complained loudly.

"Oh, the devil with this!" Geoffrey exclaimed. "We shall find the nearest posting house and hire a closed carriage for the rest of our journey. Surely that, at least, will meet with your approval?" he asked his valet sarcastically.

Dantry assured him it would.

An hour later they were on the road again, their bags strapped securely onto the back of the post chaise and four. Personally, Geoffrey considered the horses to be the slowest creatures it had ever been his misfortune to deal with, but the pace suited the valet. He, after all, had no reason to care whether they reached the Rowland household tonight or tomorrow. He had no reason to fear that this journey would prove futile. He had no reason to fear he had lost the woman he loved by his own foolish mistakes.

No, Dantry was perfectly content to sit back and let Geoffrey worry about all such things. Mind you, he voiced his opinion of having to travel so far north, particularly when he had finally had a chance to spend a Season in London with Mr. Talbot. Not that he was complaining, of course. Indeed it was a pleasure to serve a gentleman so well turned out. Still, one could not say it was particularly delightful to always find oneself buried in the countryside.

Finally, however, the Rowland estate came into sight. The house was a very large one and the grounds kept in excellent condition. This elicited a small sniff of approval from the valet.

"At least they are not entirely uncivilized here, it would appear," he conceded.

"I don't give a fig whether they are or not," Geoffrey snapped back. "My only concern is to speak to Lady Penelope and bring her to her senses."

The valet lifted his eyebrows at this forthright speaking, but he had been with Mr. Talbot long enough to know it would be wise not to comment on the matter.

It was dusk as the post chaise pulled up in front of the house. Geoffrey jumped out of the carriage and paid the post boys and coachman.

"Mind, now, my own carriage is to be delivered here the moment it has been repaired," he said.

The amount he had just paid the coachman was sufficiently generous that the fellow promised to deliver it himself, if need be.

Talbot left his valet to supervise the unloading of the baggage and strode up the front steps. The Rowlands were not expecting him, but he had no fear he would be turned away. So far as he could see, it was only Lady Penelope herself whose reaction he had to fear. Everyone else in her family seemed only too eager to thrust her into his waiting arms. He trusted this sister and her husband would do so as well.

The unfortunate servant who opened the front door seemed distinctly taken aback at the sight of the stranger at the door. "Are Mr. and Mrs. Rowland expecting you?" he asked.

"No," Geoffrey answered curtly. "But I do not think Lady Penelope will find my arrival a surprise."

The fellow bowed him in and led the way to the parlor where, he said, the family was gathering for dinner. Geoffrey tried to head directly for Lady Penelope but, as if by unspoken consent, both Miss Tibbles and a woman who he thought must be her sister, stepped in front of her.

"How nice of you to pay us a visit, Mr. Talbot," the lady said after he had been announced. "I, of course, am Mrs. Rowland. This is my husband, Mr. Rowland."

Geoffrey felt his neck cloth grow tighter. He knew he was breaking all the rules, just as Mrs. Rowland was ignoring a few of her own, but he could not stop himself.

"I wish to speak with Lady Penelope," he said tightly.

Her sister's voice was like steel as she said, "Perhaps. But it remains to be seen whether she wishes to speak with you."

At this point Mr. Rowland intervened. There was ill-concealed amusement in his voice as he said, "I presume you will wish to join us for dinner. Perhaps you would care to change your attire before you do so?"

It was phrased oh so delicately but had the effect of drawing every eye to the mud on his pantaloons and jacket. Geoffrey felt his face growing red.

"Yes. Er—that would be a very good notion."

He stammered over his words and Mr. Rowland merely smiled kindly as he rang for someone to show Mr. Talbot to his room.

"The yellow room, I think," Mrs. Rowland said thought-fully when a footman answered the summons.

Mr. Rowland started to object but did not. Geoffrey, of course, dared not ask what the jest might be. No doubt the chimney smoked or some such thing, he thought darkly, but at this time of year he scarcely cared. All he wanted was to change his clothes and return downstairs where he meant to require Lady Penelope to listen to his most rational arguments, all of which he had rehearsed over and over again as he made the journey north from London.

Not only did the chimney smoke, for Dantry had been privy to gossip about all the best and worst rooms in the house in the short time he had been below stairs, but the window needed to be repaned and a slight breeze blew through the room. At least, he told himself again, it was summer.

In an expressionless voice Dantry said, "It would seem they are not eager for you to prolong your stay, sir."

Geoffrey damned his eyes and struggled even more hastily into his change of clothes. Then it was downstairs even as Dantry tried to put the last touches on his master's evening garb.

Dinner had been set back, it seemed, and the family was still waiting downstairs. Apparently Penelope had spoken to her sister and governess because those two ladies no longer tried to block his access to her.

Still, she did not welcome him warmly. He bent over her hand and she snatched it away. He tried to tell her he had missed her.

"Indeed?" Lady Penelope said coolly. "I wonder you made the effort to follow."

"We must talk," he said, a hint of desperation in his voice.

Was that a look of hope in her eyes? Dismay? Her voice betrayed nothing but carelessness as she said, "I cannot see that we have anything to say to one another."

In spite of all his promises to himself, Geoffrey began to

lose his temper. "Perhaps you have nothing more to say to me but that does not mean—"

"Time for dinner," Mrs. Rowland said brightly. "Shall we go in? Hugh, please take Penelope, I shall go in with Mr. Talbot."

And what was there to say to that? One could not very well refuse what amounted to a command from one's hostess. Particularly when she had not invited you in the first place. Perhaps he could turn it to his advantage?

"Mrs. Rowland, I do not know what Lady Penelope has told you," he began, in a low voice that would not carry.

"Enough to know you made Penelope a very outrageous proposal, deceived her horribly, and have entirely upset her," she retorted sharply. "And if you think I shall champion your cause blindly, as my parents and my aunt have done, you very much mistake the matter."

"Mrs. Rowland, I only wish to assure you that my greatest concern is Lady Penelope's happiness." Geoffrey plowed gamely onward.

"To which end you have followed her, quite unwanted, north to my home?" Mrs. Rowland countered in the same undertone he was using.

Geoffrey felt himself coloring again. "The devil take it, Mrs. Rowland, I know she's confused, but I know, I assure you, that her happiness lies with me!"

For the first time since he had entered the house, he felt a softening in the attitude of the woman beside him.

"Perhaps," she conceded. "But it is my sister, not I, you shall have to convince of that. And how you are going to do so is beyond me."

Geoffrey sighed. He could not help himself. "Unfortunately, I am beginning to think it is beyond me, as well," he said with an air of gloom about him.

Mrs. Rowland bit her lower lip. "Perhaps after dinner," she suggested, "Hugh, my husband, will have some notion when the two of you sit together over the port."

And with that he had to be content. The table had been hastily rearranged and it was clear he was supposed to sit beside Lady Penelope, the servants having apparently grasped the situation perfectly.

But Lady Penelope chose to change places with Miss Tibbles so that Geoffrey found himself with Mrs. Rowland on one side and the governess on the other. They were both, he hoped, at least somewhat sympathetic to his mission, but he could not be absolutely certain. And in any event, it was up to him, not them, to persuade Lady Penelope to change her mind. But how he was to do that without being able to speak to her directly was, at the moment, something he simply could not fathom.

If only he knew what Lady Penelope was thinking!

Lady Penelope was thinking that she was becoming a want-wit. That her family had begun to look at her as if she were lacking in some essential ingredient of intelligence.

And perhaps she was, for she could not make up her mind about Mr. Talbot. She found herself both wanting to hold him at arm's length and at the very same time wishing to throw herself into his arms and never let him go.

She was both grateful to her sister for protecting her from Mr. Talbot's importunings and perversely annoyed that it had worked so well. She wished, above all things, to send him away. She wished, above all things, to keep him close at her side.

It could only, she told herself morosely, be that she had developed a *tendre*, perhaps even fallen in love, with the man. And it was worse, infinitely worse, than anything she could have imagined. She had been absolutely right to suspect that it would threaten to destroy her. The trouble was, now that the mischief was done, whatever could she do about it anyway? Other than absolutely refuse to allow anyone else, particularly Mr. Talbot, to know, of course. She would not allow herself to be leg-shackled to a man who would not trust her, a man who would demand her blind loyalty but refuse to share anything of consequence about himself.

Dinner was difficult. Mr. Talbot kept trying to find excuses to talk to her across Miss Tibbles. She resolutely, and quite properly, refused to indulge in such impertinent behavior. Which left her, since the table had been rearranged, with virtually no one to speak to. Miss Tibbles, after all, generally was placed at the deserted end of the table and she had usurped her place.

Still, Mr. Talbot's voice carried and she could hear him discourse on a number of topics. Wistfully she thought of how pleasant it would be if she could but allow herself to dispute him. But no, that would only allow him a chance to reply and perhaps to divert the conversation into far more dangerous channels.

Penelope scarcely picked at her food, earning an alarmed glance from the footman serving her and an admonitory glance from Miss Tibbles. But she could not bring herself to care. Somehow she had to keep Mr. Talbot from saying the things he had come here to say to her and, short of running away, which clearly did no good since he had followed her here, she thought darkly, she could not think how to do so.

When Rebecca signaled that she and Penelope and Miss Tibbles should leave the gentlemen to their port, she scrambled with unbecoming haste to leave the room. It seemed to her that Rebecca's husband, Hugh, was smiling with patent amusement, but she was far more distressed by Mr. Talbot's apparent unconcern.

Had she, in one short meal, finally succeeded in giving him a distaste of her? It ought to have pleased Penelope. Instead, she found herself thinking of ways she could undo the damage. If indeed it were not merely the product of her currently fevered imagination.

Geoffrey might have been encouraged had he been able to read the tenor of Penelope's thoughts, but perhaps not. By now he had had sufficient experience with her stubbornness to know she would stick to her guns even though her heart told her to do otherwise.

The moment the ladies were gone, he turned to Mr. Rowland, a silent plea in his eyes. Excellent fellow that he was, Hugh immediately passed the bottle of port to Geoffrey.

"It won't be easy," he cautioned. "I should guess my wife's sister to be just as stubborn as she is and that is very stubborn indeed."

Since Geoffrey had reached much the same conclusion, he did not find this encouraging. "Yes, but why?" he demanded with a scowl.

Rowland hesitated a moment before he began to speak. And when he finally did so, it was with a slow, thoughtful cadence. "I sometimes think it must be very difficult to be a twin, as my Rebecca and Lady Penelope are. They need not be identical, it seems, to form a bond so deep few others can compare or compete with it. When you add to that the fact there are five sisters in the family, well, one can imagine Lady Penelope would find herself lost now that she is the only one left at home."

"But that's just it," Geoffrey said, with no little exasperation. "If she marries me, she wouldn't be alone and she would have much more freedom than she does now. I would take her to salons, which her family never do, and she could share in my experiments! I know she would like those things. And we could both go on with our lives, just as we have before, in the ways we wish to go on the same."

Rowland stared at Geoffrey for a moment, a dazed look in his eyes, and then he burst out laughing.

"You think nothing will change?" he asked, his eyes twinkling with merriment when he could finally speak.

Geoffrey glowered. "Why not?" he demanded. "I shall

still do my experiments and Penelope may do whatever she wishes. We are both intelligent and we will both wish for and have an orderly establishment."

Rowland's lips twitched, however hard he tried to keep them still. "And when there are children?" he asked.

Geoffrey waved a hand impatiently. "There must be an heir, of course. But once that is taken care of, I see no need to have a large brood hanging about."

Rowland choked on his port. "Do you," he said, extremely carefully, "mean to cease having—er—sharing—er—why the devil do you wish to be married if you don't mean to share her bed?"

Geoffrey looked surprised. "Oh, I do. No, no, I meant there are ways to prevent excess offspring. And I am certain Penelope will be sensible enough to wish to use one of them. Once we have an heir, of course." He paused and frowned. "Well, perhaps two," he conceded. "One wouldn't wish to risk that if something happened to the first, one would be in the suds."

If Rowland had looked dazed before, he now looked positively glassy-eyed. "Have you—er—discussed this philosophy with Lady Penelope?" he asked.

"Of course not," Geoffrey said indignantly. "It would have been most improper. But she is a sensible woman. She cannot wish to have the creatures underfoot any more than I do. We will hire excellent nurses and nannies and later a tutor or governess for our children."

"Indeed?" Rowland said thoughtfully. After a moment he added, "Well, I wish you luck, Talbot. I think you are going to need it."

Surprised, Geoffrey said, "More than luck, I need the chance to speak to Lady Penelope alone."

"Oh, you need to speak to her," Rowland agreed sagely. "You need to speak with her at great length, I should say. The only question is whether or not she will let you."

And then, rising to his feet, Rowland said, "I think perhaps it is time we rejoined the ladies. Perhaps you will have your chance then."

Unfortunately for Geoffrey, Lady Penelope had already gone upstairs in search of her bed.

Chapter 22

Geoffrey rose at the hour he considered would allow him to be downstairs when he was most likely to find Lady Penelope at breakfast in the dining room. She would not, he vowed, be able to avoid him today.

Feeling rather smug, he arrived there to find himself alone and to be informed, when he asked the servants hovering nearby, that she had come and gone sometime before. With poor grace, Geoffrey filled a plate of food and forced himself to eat.

Why couldn't Lady Penelope behave as he expected her to? Why couldn't she follow the same sort of sensible schedule his mother did? Why—oh, the devil take it, why hadn't he risen earlier and come downstairs and simply waited for her in the first place?

With a snort of self-disgust, Geoffrey threw down his fork and strode from the dining room looking for all the world, the servants recounted below stairs later, as though he wished to strangle someone.

No one, it seemed, was about and the house was a veritable rabbit warren, Geoffrey thought, his temper rising as he searched for Lady Penelope. Eventually, however, he heard voices and followed them until he came to a very large room filled with a good many children, most of them clean but with the look of street urchins, for all they were here in this well-to-do household in the north of England.

Mrs. Rowland and Lady Penelope were there and each was surrounded by a circle of these children. The scene resembled, Geoffrey thought, nothing so much as a very large schoolroom. And Lady Penelope and her sister resembled the teachers. Miss Tibbles sat in a corner, a small infant on her lap, and she looked both ill at ease and yet fiercely protective of the tiny creature she held.

Talbot's first instinct was to retreat. He had no wish, after all, to thrust himself forward into bedlam. His second was to straighten his back and take a step into the room. He was not a coward and he would not, he told himself firmly, retreat, regardless of how bizarre the scene before him. He was going to have his talk with Lady Penelope.

She looked up and saw him standing in the doorway. He was staring at her with an expression of profound disapproval in his eyes and her heart sank even further.

They had never spoken of the subject of children and yet, perhaps more by what he had not said than by what he had, Penelope guessed that Mr. Talbot did not like the thought of having them about.

Well, that had been something which did not matter so long as their betrothal was merely a sham. And even when it was not, when she considered letting herself go through with a wedding after all, Penelope had thought she would not long for children either. Her sister's infants had not stirred her maternal instincts, after all.

But somehow these urchins had claimed her heart, in a way she could never have predicted. And Penelope knew, without a doubt, that if she ever married, she would want children around her.

And she would have to marry, Penelope thought with a sigh. Even she would not dare to defy society by raising children without the benefit of a husband to stand behind her. What was considered admirable, if eccentric, in Mrs. Rowland, would have been considered beyond the pale were it done by mere Lady Rebecca. Or Lady Penelope.

He was coming toward her now. She had to do something, she dare not let him say what was so clearly on his mind. Whatever her feelings for Mr. Talbot, she could not marry a man who would not be honest in his dealings with her. And one who did not like children.

Penelope looked at the children gathered around her and said in a voice that carried throughout the room, "Look! There is Mr. Talbot. Do you know he does experiments? He knows precisely how to make gunpowder and fireworks and all manner of fascinating things."

In an instant, the children were clustered around Mr. Talbot, peppering him with questions. He looked bewildered and more than a little angry with her. His eyes promised revenge later for the trick she had just played on him. But for the moment she was safe, for he was stooping down to answer their questions.

She couldn't have said when things changed. She only knew that time passed and he answered an astonishing number of questions. He eased loose his cravat and even, eventually, sat on the floor amid the children. His gestures grew extravagant and he grinned.

And then Mr. Talbot looked up at her and Penelope knew that there was the same sense of awe and astonishment in his eyes that there had been in hers the day before when she realized that she liked being surrounded by these children.

Just as she was trying to tell herself it was her imagination that she thought she beheld such a similar sentiment in Mr. Talbot's eyes, he held out his hand to her. Penelope looked around to see what her sister or Miss Tibbles might think of such a thing and discovered that at some point they must have slipped out of the room. She and Mr. Talbot were alone with the children.

Still he held out his hand to her. Penelope took a step toward him, and then another, as though held captive by something, some unexpected warmth and understanding, in his eyes. The children parted so that she could reach him and when she did she found he had gotten to his feet. But his hand was still held out to her and she placed hers inside it.

A smile tugged at the corners of his mouth and his voice was soft and gentle as he said, "I've made a dreadful muddle of things, haven't I?"

Mesmerized, she nodded.

He went on, his voice more serious than she had ever heard it before, "Will you let me try again? I promise I shall try to do better."

She wanted to say no. She wanted to guard her heart against him. But it was too late. How could she guard her heart against a man whose other hand rested on the top of a child's head and he, without thinking or even seeming to notice he did so, drew the child close.

This was a man she could love. What she did not know was if this was a man she could trust. Slowly, hesitantly, Penelope decided she would try.

She drew her hand out of his and a smile quirked at the corners of her mouth at the sight of his shocked dismay when she did so. But it did not last long. How could it when, before his expression had even fully formed, she threw her arms around his neck and hugged him tight.

"Yes, Mr. Talbot," she whispered into his ear, "I shall give you another chance."

He had to grasp her tight to keep them both from toppling over. She understood that. But it did not explain the breathless quality to his voice as he said, "I swear, Lady Penelope, you shan't regret it. But perhaps we should—er—be more discreet in front of the children?"

Instantly Penelope pulled herself away from him, blushing. He was right of course. What sort of example was she setting? But he did not seem upset with her. His smile had deepened and now he held out his hand again as he said, "Perhaps we had best tell your sister and her husband we are going back to London? And that we are getting married, after all?"

She wanted to say yes. She wanted to agree to allow him to whisk her back to London on the instant. Instead she said carefully, "I am not certain I am ready for that. I have agreed to give you another chance, not to marry you. That is still in question."

He might have argued, but the children, impatient by the delay and the nonsense going on before them, once again began to clamor for answers to their questions and Mr. Talbot allowed himself to be swept away. Penelope seized her chance and slipped out of the room. She would go for a walk and find time to think, she decided.

Later she and Mr. Talbot must have the talk they had postponed in London. She would not marry a man who would not answer her questions.

Geoffrey found her on a hillside, some distance from the house. She was sitting on a fallen log, staring out over a circle of stones.

"May I join you?" he asked quietly.

For a moment he thought she would refuse. Then she shrugged. He took it as an assent and seated himself next to, but careful not to touch her.

"You are very right, of course," he said in a conversational tone. "I ought to have been plain with you and answered your questions that day, in London."

She looked at him, then, and tilted her head, waiting. Geoffrey could see the troubled look in her eyes and it made him draw in his breath in dismay.

"It has been a habit of years to hide my father's propensities," he said quietly. "I cannot remember a time when anyone would openly speak of them. I suppose I was afraid that if I did so with you, you would send me to the rightabout. And with good cause."

He braced himself for her disdain. Instead she put a hand over his. "Tell me," she said, softly, gently, with no contempt either in her voice or in her touch or in her expression.

He did. He told her about his father's drinking and gaming and mistresses and even the times he had seen his father strike his mother. He told her about leaving the university to return home to care for his father when he was at his wildest and no one else could keep him under control.

He told her about Uncle Frederick and how he had brought Lord Talbot home that morning. He told her how much he would have owed, had Uncle Frederick decided to call in the vouchers. How he meant to hold them in case his father should try to gamble like that again.

And when he was done, Geoffrey stared at her, his face very pale, as he waited to hear what she would say.

"What are you so afraid of?" Lady Penelope asked, puzzled. "It is your father, not you, who has done these things."

His face went very white as he said, "What if I become like my father?"

Whatever Geoffrey expected it was not the smile that quirked up the corners of her mouth. Or the way her hand reached out and touched his cheek. Or the kindly condescension in her voice as she asked, "Do you like to gamble?"

"No."

"Do you like to drink to excess?"

"No. In fact I can't," he grumbled. "I become ill and pass out before ever I reach half my father's state."

"How wonderful!" She countered.

"You would not say so," he told her pithily, "if you were a man and expected to be able to drink your peers under the table."

She laughed! She had the temerity to laugh at him! But instead of growing angry, Geoffrey felt the harsh band around his heart that had been there for as long as he could remember, start to slip away. And he smiled.

"There! You see?" she asked triumphantly. "Were you like your father, you would not be smiling, you would be in a rage with me for laughing."

He took her hand and kissed the fingertips. He could not help himself. Nor the foolish grin that he could feel on his own face.

"Are you then reconciled to me?" he asked. Then, teasingly, he added, "Are you persuaded I shall be an excellent husband, after all?"

Something darkened the back of her eyes. Slowly she pulled free her hand. "I do have one concern," she said. "Do you mean to have mistresses, as your father did?"

Geoffrey gaped at her. When he did not at once answer she started to her feet, turning away her head, dismay evident in every line of her body.

Without thinking, he reached out and pulled her back to sit beside him again. When she would have twisted free, he refused to let her go.

With all the gentleness in his voice that he could muster, Geoffrey said soothingly, "What is it, my love? What are you so afraid of? I mean to have no mistresses. I cannot think I shall need one, if I am married to you."

She looked at him and he could see the tears gathered in her eyes, still unshed. "Are you certain?"

Her voice trembled and he wiped away the one tear that now trickled down her cheek. "Very certain," he replied, smiling warmly at her.

She sighed and he could feel the relief that ran through her. Before she could raise her guard again, he asked, "Why? Why were you so terrified that I might? After all, you did not fear I would be like my father in other ways."

For a moment he thought she would refuse to answer. Then she took a deep breath and began to speak, staring over his shoulder, rather than meet his eyes.

"I cannot say how old I was when I realized Papa kept a mistress. There have been a few, over the years. But I remembered vividly the first time I saw Mama cry because of it. She tried to say it did not matter to her, but Mr. Talbot, I know I could never be so sanguine. If ever you mean to keep a mistress, you had best let me know now and we shall cry off before we are shackled to one another for the rest of our lives."

Lady Penelope concluded her little speech with a note of defiance in her voice and she did meet his eyes as she said the last few words. Geoffrey chuckled. He could not help himself. And then, as her expression took on a hint of outrage, he kissed the tip of her nose.

"I shall never take a mistress," he said. "I swear it. Knowing that, will you marry me, Lady Penelope?"

Again she evaded his eyes and in cool, distant accents she said, as though thinking the matter over, "Well, I do think perhaps it would be as well if we do marry. Particularly since it seems as if you do not dislike women, after all. And we have become friends. Indeed I do like you better than most men I have met. So, yes, I think perhaps we might marry and be able to rub along tolerably well."

But Talbot was having none of it. He took her chin in his hand and forced Lady Penelope to look at him. "Do you wish to marry me?" he asked. "Not because it is sensible, or for any other bird-witted reason, but because you wish to be with me? Because you love me as much as I have come to love you?"

Her eyes opened wide. "I thought you did not believe in love, Mr. Talbot," she objected.

"I have found, much to my surprise, that I do," he grumbled.

She laughed, she could not help herself. "And I know that I love you," she told him.

This time Geoffrey could not resist a tiny crow of triumph. He drew Lady Penelope into his arms and kissed her quite thoroughly. So thoroughly that it was some time before they thought to go back to the house and tell the others.

Penelope found Miss Tibbles in the drawing room talking with Rebecca. Both sets of eyes flew to her face the moment she stepped into the room.

"I—er—that is I came to tell you that we shall be returning to London very shortly," Penelope said, feeling herself blush.

"We?"

"Miss Tibbles and I. And Mr. Talbot."

She could not meet their eyes but Penelope knew Rebecca was smiling.

As for Miss Tibbles, she grumbled, "First we are to hare off to the north, with scarcely enough time for such a journey. Then, before we have had time to settle in, you announce we are to hare back to London. I do not comprehend such bizarre behavior, truly I do not."

"But do you not think, Miss Tibbles," Penelope asked with a perfectly straight face, "that Mama and Papa would wish to know, as soon as possible, that I mean to marry Mr. Talbot, after all?"

These words produced the desired effect. Rebecca rose to her feet and ran to embrace her sister. "Truly, Penelope? This is truly what you wish?"

Penelope felt an unaccustomed shyness as she nodded and said, "Yes, it is, Rebecca."

"It is not a false betrothal this time?" Miss Tibbles demanded sternly, advancing on Penelope as well.

"No, I really do mean to marry him."

"When?" Rebecca demanded breathlessly.

Now her color was higher than ever as Penelope said, "Soon, I think. Mr. Talbot is very impatient and I, well, I find I do not wish to wait very long either."

Once more Rebecca embraced her and even Miss Tibbles grudgingly said, "Well, perhaps it does make sense to return to London then. You are quite right that your parents will wish to know. And after everything that has gone before, I must admit that the only way they are likely to believe it is if they see you in person. And a wedding does take a great deal of preparation."

Penelope could not help herself. She swept Miss Tibbles up into a hug as well. The poor governess remonstrated, but neither Rebecca nor Penelope were deceived. There was a suspicious glint in Miss Tibbles's eyes and a watery smile on her face.

"The last of us are about to be married," Rebecca teased. "Whatever will you do with yourself next?"

But before Miss Tibbles had to answer, Mr. Rowland appeared in the doorway of the drawing room. He took in the sight and drew his own conclusions.

"I—er—collect that Mr. Talbot was correct, then, in saying he is to wed Lady Penelope after all?"

As that set off a new round of exclamations, Miss Tibbles quietly slipped out of the room.

Chapter 23

Geoffrey Talbot was pardonably pleased with himself. He was going to be married to Lady Penelope, just as he had sworn to Reggie Hawthorne he would be. And with the special license he had procured, he would manage it with time to spare before the deadline he had given himself.

Why, then, he demanded, was Reggie looking so glum?

"Because it ain't like you," Hawthorne answered bluntly. "Getting leg-shackled like this."

Geoffrey hid a smile. "Well, no, one doesn't generally do so more than once. Perhaps twice, in a lifetime, at most," he agreed.

"Not what I mean. You ain't the sort to act impulsively. Never have before. Don't know what's come over you," Reggie continued to grumble.

"Perhaps I fell in love," Talbot said gently.

"Yes, well that's just it. Must have done so. And if *you* are susceptible to that sort of thing, then what chance have the rest of us to avoid the parson's mousetrap?"

Geoffrey gave a shout of laughter. He could not help himself. Hawthorne was not pleased.

"Don't see what's so funny. Even m'mother is starting to say that if you could get leg-shackled, then so could I. Ruined it for the rest of us, you know."

They were at Tattersall's and Reggie looked around, then said with a heavy sigh, "Won't see much of you here anymore, I s'pose. You'll be busy with your wife and, soon, your offspring. Won't be able to spend as much time with us. Or go out drinking whenever you wish. Or go to boxing matches anytime you please."

"Why not?" Geoffrey asked, much taken aback.

Reggie looked at him in disbelief and snorted. "Stands to reason! Why, consider Berenford. Much more the goer before he married. And what about Wilkins? Or Bartlett?"

"Yes, yes, that's enough," Geoffrey said before Hawthorne could enumerate all their married friends.

Still he was uneasy. This was not the view he had of his marriage. That was precisely why he had chosen Lady Penelope. And he didn't like to think of such a possibility now.

As for Penelope, she was not faring much better. It was bad enough that a dressmaker had been called to fit her for a wedding gown and all the new clothes her mother and aunt swore she must have. But Diana, Barbara, Annabelle, and Rebecca were all in London for the wedding. And they crowded around to give her their advice.

The only thing that was consistent, however, was the advice to let herself love Mr. Talbot and to let herself enjoy the marriage bed. Both these pieces of advice caused Penelope to color up becomingly.

Her sisters also shared, with one another, the details of their various confinements. Among them, there were now several infants and, with Barbara and Rebecca both increasing, it would soon be two more.

Talk swirled around her. Babies. Making love. Playing the role of a proper wife. It was, quite simply, more than she could bear and, in the end, Penelope fled to take counsel with Miss Tibbles.

It was the first time Penelope had ever been in the room given over to Miss Tibbles's use. The room was small but nicely furnished and Miss Tibbles had added one or two touches of her own.

There was a watercolor sketch of the canals of Venice, Italy. And another of the Lake Country in the north of England.

"They are both places I have never been but used to promise myself I would go," she explained wistfully, when Penelope asked.

"And that bit of colored grass is from Murano. My father gave it to my mother and she gave it to me. It is also from the vicinity of Venice."

For the first time Penelope looked at Miss Tibbles, really looked at her as a person and not simply her governess. And realized that Miss Tibbles was a person with hopes and dreams and fears of her own.

"What will you do," Penelope asked, "once I am married? I hadn't thought of it before, but Mama and Papa will no longer need you."

"I suppose I shall have to find another household," Miss Tibbles said reluctantly. "It will be hard. I have never stayed so long in one household before and I shall be very sorry to leave you all. Except, of course, that you have all left me. Which is just as it should be!"

"Perhaps one of my sisters—" Penelope began.

Miss Tibbles held up a hand to forestall her. "Their children are all babies and I am not in the least suited to that."

"Well," Penelope said stoutly, hoping it was true, "my parents will certainly give you all the time and help you need to find another place. And write you excellent references into the bargain."

Miss Tibbles did not answer, but instead turned the talk back to Penelope and Mr. Talbot. Penelope found herself pouring out all her hopes and fears. Miss Tibbles tried to be reassuring, but Penelope left as uncertain as when she began. All she succeeded in doing was making the governess fear that Penelope might yet cry off, on her way to the altar.

* * *

Nor did the wedding day itself help. It dawned dark and angry, with rain lashing at the windowpanes. And both Penelope and Mr. Talbot huddled deeper under their separate covers, as if hoping they could hide.

The ceremony was hideous, at least in the minds of both Penelope and Geoffrey. Against her better judgment she found herself swathed in frills and lace. He found himself being directed about as though he were no more than an actor on the stage, and one who was presumed to be wanting in wits.

They spoke their vows clearly enough, but the words were gone the moment they were over. Their hands shook as they signed their names, and each stumbled at least once on the way out of the church. Into the driving rain.

Back at Lady Brisbane's town house, where the wedding breakfast was naturally held, Penelope and Geoffrey had to endure the jests and advice and raucous suggestions everyone seemed to have to give.

When it was time to go, Penelope's maid could not find her new gloves. These, it turned out, had been packed by mistake. And then a stone tossed by an unruly child caused one of the horses to shy just as Geoffrey was about to hand her into his coach.

All in all, both Geoffrey and Penelope found themselves thinking it was something of a miracle they had managed to survive.

And yet it had not been all bad. Uncle Frederick beamed at the couple and no one said a cross word about his being there. Lord Talbot was remarkably sober and Lady Talbot hung on his arm smiling almost as if they were the newlyweds and not their son.

Miss Tibbles even hugged Penelope and charged her not to forget everything she had learned.

It was, to say the least, a trifle overwhelming.

But finally they were alone in the carriage, seated on opposite sides. Both were a little pale and neither quite knew what to say.

Geoffrey, determined to do something, switched seats. Penelope instantly scuttled away.

"Oh, no," she said. "You're not going to kiss me here."

"Why not?" he asked, taken aback.

"We are married now. Mama says that sort of thing is best kept to the bedroom," Penelope told him earnestly.

"Hang your mother!" Geoffrey exclaimed, with what might be considered pardonable frustration.

"Mr. Talbot!"

"I'm sorry, Penelope, but dash it all, we are married and we may make our own rules. It is perfectly all right for us to kiss right here. And for you to call me Geoffrey."

"It is?" she asked uncertainly, moving a little closer to him.

"It is," he said firmly, moving a little closer to her.

"Is it also all right for me to stroke the side of your face?" she asked.

She did so without waiting for his reply.

"Perfectly," he answered shakily.

"And may I kiss you?"

"Oh, yes," Geoffrey started to answer.

But he never got the chance because her lips were already reaching up to touch his, shyly, gently, with touching naiveté. And before he knew what he was about, his arms were wrapped around her and hers around him.

Of course, it was in perfect keeping with the day so far, that just as he did so, the carriage drew to a halt and it was time to climb out.

The servants were lined up to be presented to Penelope, and Geoffrey did so with as good a grace as he could manage. Then it was time to let the housekeeper show her about the house. And he had to supervise the final details of his parents' removal from London to the country house.

None of which improved Geoffrey's temper.

With one thing or another, it was late afternoon before he was free to go in search of his bride. But she was with her maid, being dressed for dinner.

Marriage, Geoffrey decided, was not what it was touted to be. Or rather, it was meeting the worst of the expectations he and his friends had once had of it.

Finally, he saw Penelope again over dinner. And she looked beautiful, dressed in a deep rose-colored gown of silk, cut daringly low, with her hair pinned in curls on the top of her head.

But even that was merely a frustrating temptation, for they were seated at opposite ends of the table, that being what his servants had decided was proper. When he would have had things rearranged, Penelope put a hand on his arm and said, with dismay, "Oh, no, pray don't disrupt everything on my account."

So Geoffrey gritted his teeth and got through dinner, talking commonplaces with his bride since there were even more servants hanging about than usual, all of whom were obviously fascinated by his new bride.

But at last they could go up to bed and Geoffrey offered Penelope his arm eagerly. Perhaps a trifle too eagerly. She turned first white, then very red, and tried to divert his interest.

He would not be diverted. Not after waiting this long to be with her.

"Don't be afraid," he assured her, thinking he knew what the trouble might be. "I shall be very gentle with you."

Now two spots of bright red anger appeared in her cheeks and she whirled away from him.

"I am not in the least afraid of you," she said defiantly. "I shall see you upstairs!"

Well, he had been clumsy, but the important thing, he told himself, watching her go, was that they were going upstairs and soon they would be in the same bed.

Geoffrey headed for his dressing room.

He found her in her bedroom, her hair down around her shoulders, wearing a night rail of the sheerest fabric he could imagine. It was white, as virginal as she was, and he trembled at the sight of her, his own robe drawn close about him.

A fire in the fireplace burned merrily, taking away the chill dampness of the night, for it had been an unusually cold and wet summer. The candlelight flickered, casting moving shadows about the room.

Geoffrey stood stock-still, thinking Penelope was the most beautiful creature he had ever seen. He must have said so aloud for she started. He waited and she came toward him. Slowly, uncertainly, with a frightened look about her eyes despite all the bravado she had shown downstairs. He reached out and tucked a strand of hair behind her ear.

"Am I truly beautiful?" she asked.

He nodded, not trusting himself to speak. He let his hand rest against the back of her neck and with his thumb stroked the side of her face.

She took a step closer. "Oh, Geoffrey, I am afraid!"

He drew Penelope into his arms, then, and kissed her, first on one eyelid and then the other. He moved to nibble at her ear, causing her to giggle, then he captured her lips with his own.

She leaned into him, oblivious to their mutual state of undress, and Geoffrey took that as a very good sign. And when she wound her arms around his neck, he knew everything was going to be all right.

Now he slipped one hand around to cup her bottom close against him, and with the other he stroked the full globe of her right breast. She moaned, but it was one of pleasure and not dismay.

And when, finally, he lifted the night rail over her head and tossed it away, her only answer was to reach for his robe to do the same.

He carried her then, over to the bed and followed her down to lay side by side upon it. She followed him, step for step, as eager to learn his body as he was to learn hers.

And when, a good time later, he felt himself spinning out of control toward ecstasy, she was right there with him. And when, at last, they came back down to earth, she was cuddled close against him.

"I didn't know," she said with something like awe in her voice, "that it was like that!"

Amused he answered, "It isn't always."

"Mama said it was something to be endured."

"I think," he said, kissing his wonderful, adorable bride, "that we can certainly do better than that."

She looked up at him, utterly at ease, with a mischievous gleam in her eyes, and said, "Shall we try?"

"Again?" he asked, pretending to groan.

A hint of uncertainty came into her eyes. "Well, whenever you are ready," she agreed.

He needed no more invitation than that. Rolling onto his back and pulling her with him, he growled, "I think, dear heart, I am ready right now!"

Chapter 24

It wasn't really that easy, of course. The nights were wonderful for Penelope and Geoffrey. But there were still all the day-to-day matters to work out. They both had brought too many fears and expectations to the marriage for it to be otherwise.

Penelope had no intention of allowing anyone, even Geoffrey, to dictate her behavior. And so it frightened her to discover that she wished to please him. It made her more determined than ever to do what she wished.

As for Geoffrey, he didn't know what to do with someone who kissed him one moment, and challenged him the next. Penelope quoted poetry at the oddest of moments and knew more about any number of things than he did. And Reggie Hawthorne's words rang in his ears, over and over again. Would his friends point at him and say he had lost his independence?

It was a very disconcerting experience, for both of them. Perhaps that was why Geoffrey took to slipping out for a while each day to get away from Penelope. Where before their marriage he would have been happy to escort her to any salon she chose, or to drive her around the park every day, now he found excuses to avoid doing so, saying she could very well manage the business herself.

Perhaps that was why, some three weeks after the wedding, when Penelope found herself alone in the house she decided to go for a walk. She saw it as something of an act of defiance, for she did not intend to take a footman with her and refused the politely expressed suggestion that she go for a drive instead.

The front door had just been opened for her, reluctantly, when three women suddenly appeared out of nowhere. Or so it seemed. The footman thought otherwise.

"Go away!" he told the women imperiously. "I've told you before, Mrs. Talbot won't see you."

"And I've told you, I am Mrs. Talbot!" a buxom blonde said, thrusting herself forward.

She was pushed aside by a creature with hair an improbable shade of red who insisted, "No, I am Mrs. Talbot."

A dark-haired beauty pushed both of them to the side and said, "You've both lost your wits. I am Mrs. Talbot and I am increasing."

The footman would have shut the door against the three women, but Penelope would not let him. She insisted that he allow the three women to enter the house.

"But it wouldn't be proper!" he said in shocked accents.

"It will be a great deal more improper to present the entire neighborhood with a present of their presumed complaints," she retorted tartly. "Now let them in and I shall see them in the study."

He sighed but did as he was bid. The three women jostled one another and complained as to precedence, but soon they were all settled in the room that heretofore had been her favorite. Penelope felt a strong headache coming on.

When they were all seated, with Penelope behind the desk, facing them, she said quietly, "I am Mrs. Talbot and I must confess I do not understand why the three of you are claiming that title."

They started talking, all at once.

"I have a child by him."

"He married me in Fleet Street."

"A proper to-do it was, all me family there."

Penelope gazed at the women shrewdly. She had a strong

feeling they believed what they were saying. And that she knew who was behind it all.

"Perhaps you are looking for Lord Talbot?" she asked.

"Lord?"

"Oh, no, ma'am, 'e was a plain mister, 'e was. Said so, 'imself."

"Not likely."

"Perhaps we are talking about a different Mr. Talbot?" Penelope persisted. "It is not, after all, such an uncommon name."

"Oh, no," the blonde said, shaking her head. "It's the Mr. Talbot wot lives 'ere. I followed 'im 'ome one night to see. Just in case like I should ever need to know."

"Er—if you considered yourself married to Mr. Talbot, why didn't you expect him to come home to you?" Penelope asked sensibly.

All three women snorted. The red-haired creature took it upon herself to explain. "He told me, he told all of us, that his family would object to the marriage. That we had to pretend, for a while, that we weren't married until he could get things in order. We didn't want him to end up penniless, you know. But we did think it a good notion to see where he lived."

"You knew each other?" Penelope asked faintly. "And you didn't think it strange he was married to more than one of you?"

The three women looked at one another in exasperation and at Penelope as if they thought she was wanting in wits. This time the dark-haired woman answered, "We met on the steps this morning. Heard about the wedding, we did, and thought we'd best come round and find out what's what."

Penelope sat back in her chair. She had a sudden notion. "Can you tell me what Mr. Talbot looks like?" she asked.

They argued over that one for several minutes. Finally,

they settled on an answer. It was one that Penelope was not expecting.

Instead of describing Lord Talbot, as she more than half expected, despite their denials, they described Geoffrey. Shaken, she questioned them to be absolutely certain on the matter. When she was done, Penelope sat back in her chair, stunned, and tried to think of what to say.

"Weren't expecting that, was you?" one of them said with satisfaction.

Penelope tried to rally herself. "Even if it is true," she said, bewildered, "what do you expect him to do?"

"Settle which one of us he's really married to."

"Do right by all of us."

"Make my child 'is 'eir."

Penelope closed her eyes. This was a nightmare. It could not be happening. But it was. Her eyes snapped open again as she realized that if any of the marriages did, by chance, happen to be legitimate, her own was not.

"You ain't about to faint, are you?" one of them asked suspiciously.

"No, no, I'm not," she said, rallying.

"Aye, that's the spirit."

"Get angry, 'e deserves it."

"Awful shock, ain't it?"

Then one of them asked the question, "Wot are you going to do?"

For a moment, Penelope didn't know. Then she did. A malicious smile curved across her face and she rose to her feet, shook out her skirts, and said brightly, "Please stay and make yourself at home. I shall direct the servants to bring you some food."

"And drink!"

"And drink," Penelope agreed. "My husband, that is to say, Mr. Talbot, should be home a little later. You will no doubt wish to stay and speak to him then."

"And you? Wot are you going to do?"

"Me?" Penelope said brightly. "I am going home!"

And with that, she turned on her heel and left the room. She spoke to the servants in the same cheerful, bright tone she had used with the three women. The servants were not pleased to hear they were to treat the three as guests, but Penelope was adamant. She threatened to sack any one of them who did not do as she said.

Then she went upstairs, put a few things into her reticule, and came back downstairs again.

"Where are you going, ma'am?" the footman at the front door stammered.

She smiled brightly at him. "Out."

"Should I call the carriage for you?"

"No, I think I should like to walk."

He wanted to stop her. He wanted to ask when she would be back. But as he was only the footman, he could do none of those things. And he had already lost the same argument earlier, so he let Penelope go. As if, he told the other servants later, there was anything else any of them could have done.

Penelope scarcely noticed where she stepped. Her thoughts were all on pretending to those she passed that nothing was amiss. And in trying to decide what she would tell everyone when she got home.

As it turned out, her mother and father were preparing to go out.

"Missed us already, puss?" Lord Westcott asked jovially. Cheerfully he set aside his hat, prepared to remain home awhile.

Lady Westcott was more perceptive, "Oh, my dear, you look dreadful! Come in here with me, where we may talk. Was he a beast? I knew I should have prepared you better for your wedding night!"

Lady Brisbane was the most perceptive of all. She watched Lord and Lady Westcott take their daughter into the drawing room and then rang the bell.

"Get Miss Tibbles," she snapped the moment a servant appeared.

Then she, too, went into the drawing room.

Penelope tried to laugh it off. To tell the tale as though it were exquisitely funny. But none of her listeners thought it was funny. Not even Miss Tibbles who came into the room when she was halfway through and carefully closed the door so that none of the other servants could overhear.

Lord Westcott threatened to horsewhip Talbot. Lady Westcott tried to tell her daughter that no doubt the women were merely Mr. Talbot's mistresses and she ought to ignore them.

Lady Brisbane had visions of Penelope back in her household again and said nothing but silently vowed to herself that the first moment it was possible, she was going to take a long journey. She was going to travel. She hadn't the slightest notion where she would travel, but she was going to travel somewhere she need not see any of her nieces, need not hear any of her nieces, need not receive news of her nieces, for as long as possible.

It was left to Miss Tibbles to show some sense. "Mr. Talbot may have an explanation," she said quietly. "There is no point in trying to come to a decision before we see if he does."

Geoffrey Talbot had no warning of the trouble ahead as he mounted the steps to his town house. He was looking forward to seeing Penelope and the moment the door opened he asked, "Where is my wife?"

His first intimation was that the majordomo said, with a perfectly expressionless face, "Which one?"

"That is not amusing," he said with a frown. "Have you been dipping into the sherry?"

"No, sir."

"Then what the devil do you mean by such an absurd question?" Geoffrey asked in exasperation.

"You will find out by going into the study, sir."

Since his majordomo would tell him nothing else, and the other servants had made themselves scarce, Geoffrey went to the back of the house where he cautiously opened the door to the study.

And promptly shut it again. A stronger man than he would have blanched at the sight. He turned to find his majordomo at his elbow. "Who are these people?" he asked through clenched teeth.

The majordomo looked up at the ceiling as he answered, "They all call themselves Mrs. Talbot, sir."

Geoffrey closed his eyes, "Where is the real Mrs. Talbot?" he asked carefully.

"That, sir, is not for me to say. We were hoping you could enlighten us."

Geoffrey damned his eyes, then said, "Where is the Mrs. Talbot who was formerly Lady Penelope, the Earl of Westcott's daughter?"

"We don't know, sir. She went out. For a walk, as she said."

Geoffrey cursed fluently for several moments. If he was impressed, the majordomo did not say so. Instead he waited impassively for Talbot to finish.

"May I suggest, sir, that you see the Mrs. Talbots now? They have been growing very impatient, over the last hour or two."

"No you may not!" Geoffrey retorted and turned on his heel.

"But sir." The majordomo gaped after him. "What am I to do with the women?"

"Anything you damn well please!" was the unfeeling reply.

Geoffrey took the stairs two at a time, hoping to find that Penelope had left him some kind of note. He could well understand that she had been so distressed that she left the house, but he hoped there was enough trust between them for her to tell him why and where she was going.

There was nothing. Or almost nothing. Only a brief note, which might have been written by anyone, tossed onto his pillow. It said only, *You seem to have been very busy.*

Geoffrey groaned. He thought about going back downstairs and speaking to the women. Instead he took the coward's way out and used the servants stairs to reach the kitchen and, from there, escape through the backyard.

Penelope must, he told himself, have gone back to her mother.

Chapter 25

There were three very different opinions as to what should be done about Mr. Talbot when he came to call. In the end, Penelope's wishes prevailed. Or rather, Penelope's wishes as shaped by Miss Tibbles.

She received him alone, a handkerchief twisting between her fingers. She would not, she swore to herself, abuse Geoffrey until she heard his side of things. How ever it may have seemed, there might be an innocent explanation for everything.

Well, perhaps not innocent, but an explanation that cleared her husband of the horrid suspicions she was feeling. He took one step into the drawing room and stopped, looking distinctly shaken.

"Pray close the door," she said, with a tolerable assumption of calm. "I do not wish everyone in this house to hear what we have to say."

He did so. Then he took another step toward her, his face very pale.

"I don't know them," he said shakily.

"Of course you don't," she agreed cordially. "Three women, all of whom can describe you perfectly, show up on your doorstep, claiming to be your wives, and you know none of them."

"I know how it must sound," he began, "but I swear—"

"Don't!" Penelope said sharply. She rose to her feet and began to pace about the room. "You lied to me about your interest in getting married. You even lied about your interest in women. You pretended to be quite the misogynist. It would seem it was an even greater lie than I had yet realized. How many other wives do you have hanging about? How many other children?"

Geoffrey Talbot was no longer pale. In fact his color had risen alarmingly. "Now listen here," he said. "I may have lied to you before, but I am not lying now. Those women are not my wives."

"No, they just think they are," she said sweetly, moving to put a sofa between them.

"I told you, I don't even know who they are," Geoffrey persisted.

"Didn't you stop to ask?"

He was pale and very earnest as he said, "No, I came straight to find you."

"That," Penelope said gravely, "was an error."

In the study of Talbot's town house, the three women were much inclined to agree.

"His high and mightiness said that Mr. Talbot had been home and left again," the blonde one said when the major domo hastily retreated after being summoned to tell them what was going on.

"No doubt after his new bride," the red-haired one snickered.

"Big mistake," the dark-haired one pronounced merrily, throwing herself into a chair. "The chit won't like it. Doubtless she'll ring a peal over his head and he won't know what to say. He really should have stopped and asked us our story."

"Couldn't face the three of us at once, no doubt." The red-haired one snickered again. "Took one look and lost his nerve and turned tail and ran."

"Well, this is the easiest money we've ever made," the blonde one said, fanning herself with her hand. "They've even fed us remarkably well, which is surprising, considering what we've been claiming."

"I do hope she forgives him," the dark-haired one said with a sigh. "It would be a pity if we broke up their marriage."

"You didn't say that when you took this job," the blonde said sharply.

"I know. I needed the money, just as both of you do. And very good money it is, too. I just hope this is the harmless prank we were promised it was."

"I'd give a monkey to be able to watch him try to sweet-talk his way out of this," the red-haired woman said.

"Or to watch her bash him over the head with something," the blonde retorted, laughing.

"Well, while we're waiting for someone to come home again, what can we do to pass the time?" the dark-haired one asked, forgetting her reservations.

Outside, across the street, Reggie Hawthorne watched the house with a growing sense of unease. It had been some time since Talbot went inside and by now he ought to have sent the girls packing. Or gone after his bride, Lady Penelope.

That part, at least, had worked well enough. She'd gone out, no doubt home to her mother. But where the devil was Geoffrey?

Geoffrey managed to corner Penelope behind the green brocade chair. As her eyes darted wildly about, looking for a way to escape, he captured her hands in his own and drew her to him.

"Do you really have so little faith in me?" he asked quietly. "That you would think I would do such a thing to you, or to any woman?"

"No," Penelope admitted reluctantly. "I know what I saw

and what they said, but in my heart I cannot believe they spoke the truth."

"Then why did you run away?"

"Because I couldn't take any chances," she said honestly. She raised her eyes to his. "You have lied to me before, you know."

He kissed her fingertips. "Only because I knew no other way to have you let me court you. But I would never lie about such a thing as this."

Really, his kisses on her fingertips were most distracting, and Penelope found it hard to think. "But what is the explanation, then, of those three women in your house, Geoffrey?"

He looked at her and grinned. "I haven't the faintest notion, my love. Why don't we go and find out together?"

When she hesitated, he added solemnly, "If you are still not satisfied after we have spoken with them, I promise I will bring you straight back here to your parents."

She swallowed hard, feeling as if she could drown in the warmth from his eyes. "Well, I suppose it could do no harm," she allowed cautiously.

They got as far as the hallway, where Lord and Lady Westcott and Lady Brisbane and even Miss Tibbles were waiting. Penelope blushed at the sight of them and whisked her hand out of Geoffrey's grasp and thrust it behind her.

"Sir, may I speak with you outside?" Lord Westcott said, taking a step forward.

"Dearest, please," Lady Westcott protested, catching her husband's arm.

"Oh, Papa, it may not be as bad as it looks," Penelope said hastily.

"May not be?" Lady Brisbane echoed, peering closely at the pair of them.

Only Miss Tibbles did not seem overwrought. She sighed and stepped forward. "I must suppose," she said dryly, "that you have managed to patch up things between you and that the supposed brides turned out to be a hum?"

"We don't know," Penelope was incautious enough to answer.

"You don't know?" her father echoed incredulously, his color starting to rise dangerously.

"I didn't stop to ask the women who they really were or what they really wanted," Geoffrey was either brave enough or foolish enough to answer.

"Well, don't you think you ought to find out?" Lady Brisbane demanded tartly.

"That's what we mean to do right now," Penelope explained eagerly.

"Oh, no, you're not to set foot in that house again until this is all straightened out," Lord Westcott snarled.

Penelope looked at her generally amiable father, startled by this change in him. Miss Tibbles seemed to be smothering a smile or laughter or both. Now, however, she judged it time to intervene.

Miss Tibbles drew herself up to her full height and said coolly, "You need not worry, Lord Westcott. I shall accompany Penelope and Mr. Talbot. If it seems wise, I shall bring her back here straightway."

That should have settled it, but of course it didn't. It was several more minutes before everyone was persuaded to agree. And then the carriage had to be brought around to convey the three of them to Mr. Talbot's town house.

Even then, as he tried to hand her into the coach, Penelope found her mother's hand clutching her sleeve. "Remember, you may always come back here," Lady Westcott said fiercely.

Just as fiercely Lord Westcott was speaking to Geoffrey. "And no tricks, now, mind! Penelope is a good girl and I won't have you making her unhappy."

The argument seemed about to start up all over again when Miss Tibbles's tart voice cut through the group of them. "If we may please be going, it is at least conceivable that I will return in time for dinner."

"Yes, Miss Tibbles," several voices said meekly at once.

Satisfied, she settled into her seat and waited for Penelope and Mr. Talbot to join her. One of these days, she thought with a sigh, someone she cared for was going to do things the ordinary way and she wasn't going to have to spend her time chasing down wraiths of scandal.

Unfortunately, it didn't look as if that day was going to come any time soon.

It didn't take long to reach the Talbot residence. And by the harried look on the face of the footman who opened the door, it was clear the women must still be there.

All three took a deep breath and then moved together toward the study. The majordomo threw open the door and announced with patent satisfaction, "Mr. Talbot. And Mrs. Talbot. And . . ."

"Miss Tibbles," the governess supplied kindly.

It really was a pity, the majordomo said below stairs, a short time later, that convention dictated he withdraw before the really interesting things were said. Still, they would have a good notion of what had transpired the moment they saw who left and who remained behind. And if they were clever, surely almost every one of them could contrive a reason to be present in or near the hallway when the routed parties left.

Upstairs, six people confronted one another and not a single one looked to be at ease. The three women Penelope had found on the doorstep promptly went into a wailing performance of their woes.

Geoffrey adjured them to stop crying and tell him what the devil was the truth.

Penelope clung to Geoffrey and wondered what she was going to do if their stories proved true.

It was, as usual, left to Miss Tibbles to resolve the mess. She circled the three women and then snorted and nodded to herself.

To the dark-haired woman she said, "I thought you

looked familiar. Lady Macbeth, wasn't it? And you, isn't your turn usually comedy? And it's been a while, but before your hair was red," she said to the third, "didn't you sing on the stage?"

All three nodded, bemused, and also more than a little pleased that someone recognized them from their performances, albeit a few years afterward.

"Well, you may as well confess as to who paid you," Miss Tibbles said briskly.

But the red-haired woman was not yet ready to admit defeat. "How do you know Mr. Talbot doesn't simply have a turn for theater wenches?"

Miss Tibbles regarded them witheringly. "I might believe it if you were each fifteen years younger. But the days when I saw you upon the stage are long over. No, even if Mr. Talbot had a passion for theater wenches, they would not be the three of you."

"Oh, very well," the dark-haired woman said, her good humor unimpaired. "We were hired by a gentleman who claimed to be a friend of yours, Mr. Talbot."

"A friend?" Penelope echoed, appalled. "You must be joking!"

But she was not. Her friends confirmed it.

"Which of my friends?" Geoffrey asked through clenched teeth.

They didn't know his name.

"What does he look like?" Geoffrey persisted.

They told him.

"Reggie!" he muttered. "Forgive me, my love," he said to Penelope, "but I need to go and see Reggie right now and explain to him just what I think of his rude jest."

But there was no need. Reggie had known the trick had failed when he saw Talbot and his bride and the other lady arrive together. Now he was admitted to the study. Instantly all six rounded on him.

"How could you ask us to play tricks on such a nice gentleman?"

"How dare you try to destroy my marriage?"

"Caught on, they have. This one recognized us."

"I told you it wasn't likely to work."

"Reggie, if there weren't ladies present, I would draw your cork, here and now. As it is, you're coming outside with me."

"No one," Miss Tibbles said in her sensible voice that somehow managed to bring all of them to silence, "is going anywhere just yet. I think, sir, it would be best if you explained yourself. Before Mr. Talbot regrettably—er—draws your cork."

"And darkens his lights," Geoffrey added with a growl.

Now Reggie looked distinctly alarmed. He hastened to explain. "Didn't think there would be any harm in it. Wanted to see if she deserved you. Would trust you. Would send these girls to the rightabout. And she didn't."

Talbot closed his eyes, then opened them again. "Reggie, it is obvious that my marriage has unhinged you."

"Not me," Reggie grumbled, "m'mother. Determined to see me married. Don't want to be married. Don't want things to change. And if I could show her your marriage a mistake, she might think my marriage would be a mistake."

"Perhaps, Mr. Hawthorne," Miss Tibbles suggested gently, "this would be a good time for you to travel? To broaden your mind, as it were? Then your mother could not always be troubling you."

"Don't want to leave London," Reggie retorted. "Like it here."

For a moment there was an unhappy silence. Then Penelope said slowly, "Well, if you don't want to leave, what about your mother? Could you persuade her to travel?"

Hawthorne looked at Penelope, his mouth hanging open. And then he said slowly, "M'mother has talked of wanting to see Paris. And Rome." He began to nod vigorously. "By

Jove, I think it might work. She don't mind change. I do, but she don't. Thank you! Thank you very much! I think I'll go home and suggest it to her right now."

He turned to go and Geoffrey stopped him. Reggie looked at his friend in alarm. But all Talbot said was, in the gentlest of voices, "Reggie, you are going to take these women with you."

He looked aghast. "I can't take them home to my mother!" he protested. "She'd never leave me alone if she thought I was consorting with their sort."

"Reggie, I don't give a damn where you take these women," Geoffrey said, "but you are taking them out of my house. Right now."

Well, even Hawthorne could see the sense in that and they were eager enough to go, pausing only long enough to bestow either good wishes or advice or both upon the newly married pair.

Penelope watched it all with bemusement. And then it was Miss Tibbles's turn to leave. Her eyes seemed suspiciously moist as she rubbed her spectacles with the fabric of her skirt. And she would not meet Penelope's eyes as she said, "I do wish the pair of you happiness, my dear. And do try, both of you, not to be so impetuous in the future."

And then the two of them were alone. With the whole of the evening ahead in which to reconcile. It was a far more pleasant prospect than she would have guessed possible, just a few months before.

Penelope turned to her husband and smiled. About to say something, Geoffrey let out his breath instead and held his arms open. Without a second's hesitation, she went into them. And then he whispered a most improper suggestion in her ear, she laughed and made not the slightest objection.

Together they went upstairs.

Epilogue

In the study of the London town house, Mr. and Mrs. Talbot stood over the desk, their heads bent together, studying a series of figures on a piece of paper.

All around them, open books lay scattered about the room, places marked with anything handy. A box of unopened books stood ready for their perusal.

Down in the kitchens, a lively discussion was going on between the upper servants. It was pointless, they agreed, to announce, yet again, that it was time to eat. Instead, they decided to send up a tray with nourishing food to the study for the master and mistress.

Back upstairs, Penelope and Geoffrey had no notion of the concern their servants felt for them. They were still deep in the midst of their discussion.

"It is no good," Penelope said, "we haven't enough ingredients to do the experiment that way. What if we make this change?"

"Yes, and alter this part as well?" Geoffrey chimed in eagerly.

They made a few more changes, then looked at one another, their eyes brimming with excitement.

"Wait until Berenford hears what we mean to do," Geoffrey said mischievously. "He was certain we could not make this work. Where the devil is his letter? I must answer it right away and tell him what we are thinking of doing."

With a slight sense of guilty dismay, both Penelope and

Geoffrey looked around the room the servants were not allowed to clean.

"You take that pile," Geoffrey suggested, "and I shall take this!"

Within moments they were both busy at the task. Suddenly Penelope gave an exclamation of dismay. Geoffrey hurried over to her side. "What is the matter, my love? A spider amidst the books again?" he asked teasingly.

"It only happened once," she snapped back. "You know in general I am not so missish. No, it is just that I have found yesterday's mail which we have not yet read. And there is a letter from Barbara. I can scarcely read her writing but she seems to be saying that Miss Tibbles, my old governess, is behaving scandalously in Bath. But that could not possibly be true! Could it?"

"I shouldn't think so!" Geoffrey answered briskly. "She must be mistaken, though I suppose you could write her for more details." Then, cautiously, he asked, "Are there any other unread letters?"

There were, of course. This time it was Geoffrey who made the discovery. Guiltily he held up a letter that came from his parents. It was still sealed.

"You open it," he said.

"Coward!" she teased.

Nevertheless, Penelope took the letter and read it silently as Geoffrey shifted from foot to foot. "Well?" he said when he could stand it no longer. "Has my mother complained about our housekeeping? Did my father go hunting and shoot one of the baggers by mistake again? What the devil does she say?"

"Your mother has written a wonderful letter," Penelope chided him. "As for your father, I don't think he has gone out hunting of late. Or done anything to cavil about. Your mother writes that he is trying to persuade her to learn to play billiards."

Geoffrey gave a sigh of relief. Then, with a worried look in his eyes, he said, "Will you mind being under the same roof with them, when we go to visit next month?"

Penelope hesitated. "I own I did worry, the first time we did so, that you and your father would constantly come to cuffs. And that your mother would regret retiring to the country with him. But it has worked out amazingly well. Of course," she added, her voice taking on a teasing note, "it does help that they have such a rambling old house a dozen couples could live there and not see one another unless they so chose."

"Good," he said with another sigh of relief. "But we still have to find that letter from Berenford."

"Instead of wasting time looking for the letter," Penelope countered, "why don't we just invite him to come along when we do the experiment? He will no doubt repeat whatever he said and you can dispute it then."

"Capital notion!" Geoffrey agreed.

"Yes, but when?" Penelope asked, with a frown. "We are giving a salon tomorrow evening and the day after we are pledged to attend a lecture and the day after that Aunt Ariana expects us to come for dinner."

"I don't suppose we could do it here? Out in the back?" Geoffrey suggested hopefully.

Penelope sighed and shook her head. "You know very well how upset our neighbors got when the last experiment went awry. I told you mixing those two solutions would not do! And I do not think they would be pleased if we tried this one here. If it goes wrong it could be even worse."

"I have a shrew for a wife," Geoffrey said teasingly. "She will not let me do a thing that I wish!"

But he softened the words with a grin and a kiss to the tip of Penelope's nose. She grinned in return. "You shan't divert me that way," she warned. "We must decide where and when to do the experiment."

Eventually they settled on a place and a day. Geoffrey

started to sit down to write Berenford and paused. "I am so very glad you are my wife," he said with loving eyes as he looked at Penelope.

He held his arms open and she came into them, meeting his kiss with patent pleasure. Some time later, with her head resting against his chest, she said quietly, "I am so very glad that you found a way past all my defenses and persuaded me that marriage would not be such a terrible thing after all."

That, they both agreed, deserved another very long kiss and it was some time before the letter to Berenford got written.

Author's Note

We are coming to the end of the series and I will hate to take my leave of the Westcott family! In the final book, *Miss Tibbles' Follies*, I will have one last chance to help Miss Tibbles find love and happiness.

Colonel Merriweather and Miss Tibbles are two individuals accustomed to issuing commands and being obeyed. But what happens when they turn their attention to one another?

I cannot wait to begin writing and find out!